Praise for BREATHE
A Ghost Story

'a true ghost story – the kind that lays its cold fingers on you, grips tight and doesn't let you go even when the last page has been turned . . . Wonderfully spine-chilling . . .'

The Bookseller

'Readers . . . will be gripped and spooked.'   *TES*

'An astoundingly creative story, with some truly scary moments . . . the remarkable way in which McNish develops the theme of breathing, including an acutely well-drawn representation of Jack's chronic asthma, and you find yourself with a multi-layered story that will genuinely unnerve the reader, in a way so many ghost stories fail to do.'

Books for Keeps

'Just the thing for adolescents in search of something engagingly horrible . . . startling.'   *Independent*

'Such is McNish's skill that when you read of the young hero Jack's asthma attacks, you'll find your own breathing feels constricted. He evokes the same empathy when dealing with the ghosts who haunt Jack, taking us into the realms of inventiveness that are his trademark. Breathtaking.'

Guardian

'*Breathe* is a brilliantly inventive ghost story, compellingly written. It is spine-chilling, disturbing and truly frightening. A real page-turner.'   *Booktrust*

'An intense supernatural sto~   ~ haunts the reader'

Funday Times

'A genuinely spooky ghost story that leaves you breathless'

'Scary, disturbing and intense . . . a thoroughbred among haunted house tales . . . McNish knows how to keep the reader dangling, ensuring you'll be hard-pressed to put this down once you've started. An excellent, if unsettling experience'

'Jack's susceptibility to frightening asthma attacks matches the consumptive sufferings of a long dead girl. Readers aged 10 and above will be gripped and spooked.'

'A terrifyingly well-written and disturbing story . . . the ending is moving testament to the transforming power of love.'

'Nothing is as simple as it seems until the very last explosive climax. A brilliant winter warmer.'

'This title is pure, traditional ghost story. It sets out to chill and it does . . . a suspenseful page-turner . . . a spine-tingler.'

'If you're after a seriously spooky story, this is the one for you . . . a truly terrifying tale.'

'Gripping in its claustrophobic intensity . . . An irresistable page-turner.'

'You shouldn't really read this before you go to sleep'

'A brilliant ghost story . . . The descriptions are wonderfully vivid'

BREATHE

A ghost story

CLIFF McNISH

Chapter head illustrations by Geoff Taylor

Orion
Children's Books

First published in Great Britain in 2006
by Orion Children's books
This paperback edition first published 2007
by Orion Children's Books
a division of the Orion Publishing Group Ltd
Orion House
5 Upper St Martin's Lane
London WC2H 9EA

An Hachette UK Company

7 9 10 8 6

A catalogue record for this book
is available from the British Library

ISBN – 9781 84255 559 0

Printed in Great Britain by
Clays Ltd, St Ives plc

The Orion Publishing Group's policy is to use papers that
are natural, renewable and recyclable products and made
from wood grown in sustainable forests. The logging and
manufacturing processes are expected to conform to the
environmental regulations of the country of origin.

Author's note: The extract on p. 40 is from
'The Unseen Playmate' by Robert Louis Stevenson.
The extract on pp. 125 – 6 is from 'A Nonsense Rhyme'
by Charles Henry Ross.

www.orionbooks.co.uk

For the Dani family

Also by Cliff McNish

Contents

One

The Ghost Children

Lonely, invisible, and still wearing the clothes they had died in: the ghosts of four children were in this house. Something had disturbed their spirits, and now they were rising slowly up from the cool darkness of the cellar.

The cellar was closed, but that did not stop them; their bodies, though unable to pass through solid objects, could squeeze into small spaces or under the crack of an old door.

Ann, the eldest, fourteen when she'd died, emerged ahead of the others. The first thing she did was shield her eyes against the intense glare of summer sunshine. As she raised her arm, the light reflected off her thin white cotton slip. It was her death robe – the only item of clothing she'd been able to bear against her feverish skin in the last days before scarlatina killed her sixty-five years earlier.

Once Ann was sure the corridor was safe to enter, she

called the others out of the cellar gloom. Oliver floated ahead, while the youngsters, Charlie and Gwyneth, held her hands.

Ann led them in a slow-motion, stately drift towards the front of the house. The ghosts never walked. They couldn't. Being almost weightless, the moment they pushed off with their feet the least little draught wafted their bodies to and fro like dry, dizzy leaves around the house. With patience, they'd learned to guide themselves on the breezes stirred whenever a door or window was opened. But the house had been locked up and empty for weeks, making today's journey a particularly tricky one. Only Oliver could easily ride the sluggish tides of air around the rooms at such times.

Gliding along the corridor, Ann remained alert to danger. She never stopped calculating the fastest escape route if they had to hide from *her*. Oliver, twelve years old when he'd died, was less careful. Part of him enjoyed the risk of travelling between rooms, knowing he was quick enough to flee if he had to. Drifting impatiently ahead of the others, he rose halfway up the pane of glass in the front door.

'Don't rush,' Ann hissed. 'You know it's dangerous. You're stirring up too much air. *She'll* notice.'

'Keep up then,' Oliver hissed back. 'If you want to miss whoever's arriving, that's up to you. Anyway, stop worrying. She's asleep. She hasn't woken for ages.'

'But if someone new is coming, sooner or later she's bound to want to see who it is. You know that. Especially if it's a child.'

'So what. Let her wake. Let her freak out for all I care. She'll never catch me.'

2

'But she might catch *us*,' Ann growled. 'And you know what she'll do to us if she does.'

Seven-year-old Gwyneth wasn't listening to this argument. She couldn't wait to see who the new arrivals would be.

'Girls! Make it girls!' she whispered, squeezing Ann's hand. 'If there are girls this time, will I be able to play with them?'

'Shush now,' Ann said gently. 'You know you can't play with the living.'

Gwyneth crossed her fingers anyway, adjusted her yellow nightie and shook the worst of the cellar dust out of her mousy hair. Her spirit had been stuck in the house for forty years, waiting for someone new to play with. 'Please be a girl,' she chanted. 'Please be a girl . . .'

The second ghost boy, Charlie, looked small and weak, even next to Gwyneth. Aged eight, a disease in his final months had taken so much weight off him that now, in death, his blue paisley pyjamas hung like baggy drapes from his narrow shoulders. Trying not to sound desperate, he asked, 'Is there a boy, Oliver? Can you see yet?'

From the door, Oliver winked playfully at Ann.

'Nah. Just girls, I reckon. Disappointing, eh?'

'Girls?' Frustrated, but not wanting to show it, Charlie waited for more information.

'Yeah,' Oliver said. 'Unusually ugly ones as well. I'm not sure you'll even want to see them, Charlie boy. They're skipping towards the house.'

'Really?' Charlie blinked. He always believed everything Oliver said. 'I can't hear them . . .'

'How many, Oliver?' Ann demanded. No one was

skipping, and it couldn't only be girls. There had to be at least one adult; she'd heard the car pulling into the drive.

Oliver laughed. 'Just as eager to know as the little 'uns, eh?'

Secretly, though, the sound of the car's engine unnerved him. He'd been in the rear seat of his father's Audi when it veered off the road all those years ago. Not the biggest of crashes, but Oliver hadn't been wearing a seat belt and his short blond curls weren't sufficient to protect his skull. He'd been dressed in a red T-shirt and sandals for the beach that day. Once he was dead he discarded the sandals. No need for them. Like the other ghost children, he couldn't leave; he was imprisoned in the house. Oliver was the most recent dead arrival. He'd only been in the house eleven years – hardly any time at all.

Staring nonchalantly out of the window, he said, 'Well, since you're all so excited, let's see what we've got then. They're just getting out of the car now. Mm. Could be anything. Wait!' He slapped his head in mock surprise, knocking himself back from the door. 'Well, hey, I was completely wrong. It's not a bunch of skipping girlies at all. It's a hell of a lot better than that. Get ready for some fun, Charlie.'

'A boy!' Charlie exulted.

Gwyneth squealed with disappointment, and demanded that Ann sing her a rhyme – her usual response to frustration or fear.

'Not now,' Ann said. 'Quickly, jump up with me.' Feeling a current of air seep under her that only Oliver had been skilful enough to catch earlier, she gathered Gwyneth and Charlie in her arms, and they wafted up the front door.

4

Oliver made room for them alongside him, and the four ghosts pressed their bodies against the glass.

Ann was just as excited as the others. It had been years since any young people had come to stay. The last person in the house, an elderly woman, had lived alone for more than twenty years, leading a quiet, bookish life. The ghost children had grown fond of her, but it wasn't the same as having a real living child around.

'Here he comes,' Oliver whispered.

A boy was approaching the house.

Ann drank him in: longish auburn hair, medium height, what looked like green eyes. About twelve years old, she estimated. Not bad looking. He sauntered down the garden path, idly kicking the frame of the garden's rusted old swing.

'Don't even think about it,' a woman, obviously his mother, warned. 'I mean it, Jack. That thing's falling to bits.'

Jack, Ann thought. She turned the name round in her mind, getting used to it. Then she glanced at the swing. Was it dangerous? Possibly. No one had bothered using it for at least a generation. Since the seat was still attached to its ancient rotted ropes, Jack was sure to try it. Boys were like that. He'd pretend not to be interested, but one day, when he had nothing better to do, and his mum wasn't looking, he was bound to sit on it. Ann hoped the swing was safer than it looked. She didn't want Jack dying and suffering the same fate she and the others had done. Whatever you do, please don't have an accident, she thought. Don't die anywhere near this house.

She shook her head, studying Jack's features again. Nice eyes, she decided. Definitely green. Thick lashes. He looked interesting. Of course, after the acute boredom of the last twenty years, *anyone* new would be interesting.

Oliver studied Jack's mother. He'd never admitted to the others how much he missed his own mum, but he did miss her, and as this one stepped closer he partially hid his face from Charlie to conceal his emotions. Stupid, he thought. Ridiculous. She's not like your old mum at all. Taller for a start. Slimmer too, and younger – mid-thirties, he guessed. Her dark brown hair was arranged in a loose pony tail. Oliver watched it bob up and down as she trod carefully up the small loose stones of the footpath. I've seen you before, he murmured to himself. Oh yes.

Six weeks earlier he'd been floating around the house when Jack's mother first came to view the property with the estate agent. The second time he saw her she was carrying a few boxes of personal possessions into the house, and a stiff breeze followed her inside. The doors and windows had been shut for so many weeks since the old woman's death that Oliver hadn't expected anything like that – the rapture of a breeze. It blew like a blessing in through the front door and out into the corridor beyond, the dust rising up from the floorboards like a vapour and Oliver, rising with it, rippling and fluttering, wafting back and forth as if he had been blown in like an accident from outside, rather than stuck here all these years. In that moment, Oliver had briefly remembered what it felt like to be alive again.

He turned his attention back to Jack, sizing him up. White trainers. Jeans. No dad with him, either –

interesting. As they made their way down the garden path, Oliver noted the easygoing, close relationship Jack obviously had with his mum, and felt envious.

'He looks like an idiot,' he whispered to Charlie. 'Don't you reckon?'

'Definitely,' Charlie answered.

While Gwyneth was around, Charlie kept up a grin, but actually he felt deflated. Jack was more Oliver's age than his. Not only that, but Oliver was bound to ignore him for weeks, until he got bored with following Jack around. That meant Charlie would have to make do with playing with Gwyneth. He didn't mind that, but he hated it when Oliver excluded him from anything.

Gwyneth rested her chin on Ann's arm, feeling sorry for herself. Not fair, she thought, glancing jealously at Charlie. Not one girl to play with or even look at.

Then something made Gwyneth gasp and forget all about other girls. Because when Jack reached the front door he did an odd thing: he twisted his head and glanced up towards them.

All the ghosts noticed it. Ann shrank instinctively against the magnolia-painted wall, then laughed at herself. She knew they couldn't be seen or heard. Oliver had once proved it beyond any doubt, spending hours amusing the others by drifting up and down the old woman's legs, yelling at the top of his voice.

'He . . . didn't see us,' Charlie gasped. 'He couldn't have . . . could he?'

'No, I think he just looked up in our general direction,' Ann replied, trying to stay calm.

'But let's make sure, eh?' Oliver said. 'I'll nip in front of him when he comes through the door. Right in front of his eyes. See what happens.'

More excited than she could remember being for years, Ann nodded. The rest of the ghost children positioned themselves with her against the wall behind the door, away from any draughts, and waited.

Voices outside. A key turned in the lock.

Oliver clung tightly to the door frame, judging the right time to let go.

The mother came in first. Jack, wiping his trainers on the mat, kept the ghosts waiting a little longer. Then he stepped over the threshold.

Oliver, letting go of the door frame, saluted him. 'Hiya!' he said loudly, blowing past Jack and waving his arms. The breeze instantly picked Oliver up and threw him into the wall at the back of the corridor, but he used every trick he knew to navigate back fast. He couldn't wait to see Jack's reaction. Nor could the others.

The four of them avidly watched Jack's expression as he stepped into the house.

Two

The Drop of Blood

Jack blinked a few times, gazing around the hallway, sure he'd seen something. Then he shrugged, dismissing it. A shadow. Or nothing at all.

Trudging inside, he walked straight into one of the exposed wooden ceiling beams.

'Who used to live here, anyway?' he groaned. 'Midgets?'

His mother, Sarah, laughed. 'I warned you about the low ceilings.' In one long glance she took in the narrow corridor and smelled a certain distinctive odour she always associated with old houses. The estate agents haven't even bothered cleaning the place properly, she thought. Typical.

A lounge opened up to the left of the hallway. Jack walked straight inside, knelt beside one of the low-backed sofas and caressed it in several places. Sarah smiled. Just Jack being Jack. She watched as he wandered happily around the room, stroking the cracked mosaic tiles of the open fireplace, and everything else in sight, lightly running his fingers across the surfaces, getting to know the place.

'I love it,' he said, brushing the back of his hand against a threadbare stool. 'Mum, I really do.'

'Thought you might.'

The way people who had once lived in houses conveyed themselves to Jack – through tiny, fleeting trace memories left in furniture – was an oddity Sarah didn't pretend to understand. Nor had she ever grown used to it. As she led him into the dining room, Jack let his fingernails linger and scrape against the door frame before he went inside, and when he saw the antique table and chairs he reacted as if they were Christmas presents. Sarah grinned. A dilapidated farmhouse, creaking on its wonky two-hundred-year-old foundations. Yes, it was absolutely perfect for Jack. And that was good, because she'd wanted to spoil him. He'd been through enough stress lately; three huge asthma attacks in one year – and then what happened to his dad.

She nudged him up a steep flight of stairs leading from the ground-floor corridor to the first-floor landing.

'Three bedrooms,' she announced. 'Originally four – one's been converted into a bathroom, but the others haven't been modernized much. And this room' – she tapped the door – 'is all yours.'

Jack reached out to grip the door's brass handle. As soon as he did, there shot through him a sensation of hard, arthritic hands. An old person's hands? It was an unusually clear feeling. Generally he just got a vague impression of who'd last been in a room, not their age.

Fascinated, he went inside. He fingered the soft, heavy folds of the velveteen curtains, then stepped across to the pine bed. He kneaded the slightly lumpy mattress. The impressions were incredibly vivid. The only time he'd experienced anything like this was when he'd touched the wall his dad had been slumped against, just before the ambulance took him away.

Did someone die here recently? Jack wondered. Is that why I'm sensing this all so clearly?

He glanced across at the small bedside table, and saw a photo of his dad. His mum had obviously put it there, knowing he'd only ask for it. It was the snapshot of the three of them together, standing on the porch, about seven months ago, just before it happened. Stephen, Jack's dad, was smiling. He looked healthy. He *had been* healthy. There'd been no warning of the heart attack to come.

Sarah dropped her hand on his shoulder.

'Let me see.'

She wiped a thumb print from the glass, gazing at the picture for a while, then carefully put it back.

'Just me and you now, eh?' she whispered, resting her hand on Jack's cheek. 'A fresh start. Us against the world.'

'Yes,' Jack said thickly.

'It'll be fine,' she murmured, her hand still there. 'We'll make a real home here. It'll be OK. *We'll* be OK. You'll see.'

For the next few hours Jack helped her unpack and tidy up. In the afternoon, Sarah decided to make up the open fire in the lounge. 'A house warming,' she said. She used sticks and firelighters to get the fire blazing, then perched herself diffidently on one of the squat sofas. For a time both of them gazed into the flames, talking about nothing in particular, just getting familiar with the atmosphere of the place. A grandfather clock ticked noisily away, shattering the peace of the house every fifteen minutes with its sweet chimes.

Jack's hands roved all over the arms of his chair. They patted the fabric, stopped, slid on, always seeking something – a constant, reflective, elegant motion. Sarah was used to it, but the habit had cost him dearly. Few close friends, for a start. Who wanted to be seen hanging around with someone whose hands wouldn't stay still? Jack could control himself if he had to, but whenever he was around old furniture the second he lost concentration his hands went wandering. Today, though, there was an extra intensity about the way his long fingers travelled. They seemed more sure of themselves.

'So what's the verdict?' she asked. 'I had to search forever to find a place as old and run-down as this.'

Jack grinned. 'It's good, Mum. It'll do just fine.'

She grinned back. 'You've always wanted this, haven't you?'

'What do you mean?'

'A *really* old house. One, preferably, you know, totally falling to bits.'

Jack nodded ruefully. 'Yeah, something . . . I don't know . . .' He shrugged, unable to put his feelings into words.

'Something ancient,' she said, and they both laughed.

Later, while Sarah drove to the nearest town to find a supermarket, Jack slipped back upstairs. Everything about his bedroom – the coving, the old flock wallpaper, even the scuffed bare floorboards – intrigued him. He levered his toes up and down on the wooden boards, enjoying the creak. Lots of people had walked around this room.

But it was the bed that attracted him most of all. He let his hands wander over it, plumping the pillows, stacking them on top of each other. That seemed right, for some reason. He made an adjustment of the bedspread, folding it across in a crisp triangle. Every morning, the last person who slept here put the sheets across like this, he suddenly realized. Neatly. Even though there was no one else to see it. And no duvet. Whoever slept here preferred blankets. *She* preferred blankets.

It was a woman.

She died here, he suddenly realized. An old woman. In this bed. And she was lying here, where my hand is, when it happened.

Jack trembled, shocked that he could discover so much. Except for the traces left by his dad in the old house, he'd never picked up the presence of death before. It was as if his own dad's death had sensitised him to them. His fingers strayed over the mattress, telling him more. Three blankets in winter, he realized. And two sheets. That's what she liked. She lay between two sheets on the evening she passed away.

He jumped away from the bed, frightened by the clarity of it all. He didn't like this. It reminded him far too much of what had happened to his dad. Not wanting to think about that, he left, glanced around his mum's room, then checked out the third bedroom. It was the smallest bedroom in the house, unused for years, and empty. Even so, he felt drawn to it. Why? Was there more death here?

The door handle was a recent replacement. No inter-esting sensations, save a trace from that arthritic hand again. Jack was sure the hand belonged to the woman who had died now. She was in pain for a long time, he thought. But only slight pain. And she opened doors gently. She was a mild woman. A quiet one. He felt the hesitant shuffles of her small feet on the floor, and smiled.

Then, holding his breath, he stepped cautiously into the third bedroom.

In one corner there was an ancient cobweb. In the middle of the cobweb lay a mummified spider. It was as Jack set off across the room to study it more closely that a strange tingle made him stop. It felt as if he had touched something – or something touched him. The sensation was like the nail of a small finger brushing across his back.

With every hair rising on his neck, he turned.

To see only the doorway and the empty landing.

You little baby, he thought. Stop being jittery. There's nothing there.

The room had a single low rectangular window, barely large enough to contain the face of a child. Jack felt drawn to it, but the view was disappointing. Just some fields, the edge of a wood and a horizon. A weed-ridden back garden stared sadly up at him. There were no other houses or people in sight. The farmhouse was isolated by acres of wheat and barley fields.

The window was dust-encrusted. Before clearing it for a better look, Jack reached into his jeans, whipped out his inhaler and took a squirt. Dust didn't normally set off his asthma, but he'd had a bad attack recently, and didn't want to take any chances. Then he put his face up against the cold glass. As soon as he did so he stepped back, stunned.

Another person had also been here, face pressed up against the window. Someone who'd been here for a long time. Someone who *stared out* for years and years.

'Who were you?' Jack said out loud. 'What were you doing here so long on your own? Were you a prisoner in this room?'

A spattering of raindrops dribbled down the window pane. Without him being aware of it, Jack's hands made full contact with the glass. When he touched the frame, the taste of blood came into his mouth.

With a cry of disgust, he jumped back, but his hands were already guiding him to the floor. They stroked the bare wooden boards feverishly, rubbing the skin nearly raw on his thumb. Something was here, next to the window, he realized. A chair? Yes. This is where you sat, isn't it? he thought. For years, you hardly left a chair.

He nervously returned to the window, gripping the frame tightly with one hand. His other hand settled on the floor, making slow purposeful motions.

And suddenly, as he looked up, Jack saw not the window but a slim woman, wandering between flowers in the garden. But it was not the present garden, it was that of the distant past, and the woman wore an old-fashioned dress that was black, as if she was in mourning. Beneath the dress she wore outdoor stockings and hob-nailed boots, and she was young and very much alive, this woman, perhaps twenty-five years old, and Jack's heart leapt, wondering who she was. Her thick dark hair was stuffed under a bonnet, also trimmed with black. It was the same garden

Jack knew, too, but larger, given over mostly to crops. Chickens scratched about in a clear patch, and there was a pig.

As Jack waited for something to happen, a little girl emerged from a side entrance to the cottage. She skipped down the garden path.

It's *her*, he realized. The person from the chair. He was sure of it.

The girl wandered between different and delicate flowers, throwing weeds into a front bib tied to her black pinafore. She and the woman – so obviously her mother now – laughed occasionally while they worked, but Jack couldn't tell what they were saying. A brown-and-white terrier puppy followed the girl around, wagging his tail with excitement. It was a warm summer's day, and at one point a breeze lifted up the girl's lengthy auburn hair, making her giggle. Her mother caught several strands, wrapping them round a thumb and two fingers of her hand. Then she bent down to kiss her.

Back in the empty bedroom, still touching the floor and window-frame, Jack felt happy, without knowing why. Gradually he realized it was because the girl and her mother, in that moment, had been so happy.

Then a cough started up in the girl's throat.

It began innocently enough, just a little cough that would stop any second. But from the first hint of it, the first clearing of the girl's throat, her mother was horrified. Jack couldn't understand why. She grasped her daughter, pulling her into the folds of her dress.

The girl continued to cough. In embarrassment, half-laughing, she hid her face in her hands. But the cough wouldn't stop. It just kept on and on, and finally she was coughing so hard that she could barely catch her breath. She fought to get away from her mother, suddenly, to reach some space, some air, lifting her head, mouth open wide, and briefly recovered. Then another coughing fit overtook her, worse than the last, and her eyes were wide, moist and frightened.

'Mother!'

It was the first word Jack heard clearly, and it came out of the little girl more like a scream than a word. It made him want to scream as well, it was so heartfelt, and as she screamed a second time something splashed from her mouth.

Something.

The coughing fit was at an end.

The girl sank into the arms of her mother until she had her breath back. Then she felt the sticky area around her mouth.

'Mother?'

The girl lifted her hand to show her.

'It's nothing,' her mother rasped, not even looking at it, deliberately not looking. 'Be still, now. It's nothing at all.'

The girl glanced inquisitively down at her hand.

In the middle of her palm was a single bright red drop of blood.

Three

The Allure of the Dead

'Jack?' said a frightened voice behind him.

With the taste of blood still in his mouth, Jack got up shakily from the floor, both arms trembling.

Sarah stood at the door.

'Come here,' Jack said huskily.

'What were you doing?'

'Just come here, Mum.'

Sarah had never seen Jack behaving like this before – his hands wild, so animated.

'Who do you think might have been in this room?' he asked.

'It's tiny.' She shook her head. 'It's hard to imagine anyone staying here.'

'Too small for an adult, yes. But what if it was a child? A little girl.'

'A girl?'

'Someone stuck here, who looked out of this window for years. Someone who *could* do nothing else, she was so ill.'

'Jack . . . what . . . what makes you say that?'

He rested his fingertips on the windowsill. The bitter aftertaste of blood was still in his mouth.

'There's something else, Mum. Do you know what happened in the house just before we came?'

'What do you mean?'

'I mean, if a woman died here? Died in my room.'

Sarah tried to make sense of what Jack was saying. The estate agents hadn't mentioned anything about a recent death in the property. If they had, following his dad's death, this was the last place she'd have brought Jack.

'There are dead impressions all over this house,' he said. His nose was slightly blocked, so he automatically took another dose from his inhaler. 'What other rooms haven't we looked in yet? There must be some.' He strode past her.

Sarah hesitated, unsure what to do. This was just the sort of behaviour Jack had shown when his dad died – rushing all over the house, desperate to be close to everything he'd ever touched. That was understandable; he was just coping with grief in his own way, and while dealing with her own sorrow she'd done everything she could to help him through it. But as the months passed Jack had withdrawn further from the real world, not returned to it. He'd taken to staying day and night in his dad's study – where the traces were strongest and most numerous. On some days he'd only emerged to eat. On others, he wouldn't eat at all.

Sarah had brought him to this house to get away from all those old associations, not to revive them. Oh no, she thought. It's happening all over again. Jack's just moved his behaviour from there to here . . .

She held him. 'Listen to me . . .'

Jack shrugged her off. 'Mum, I'm OK. I just . . . where haven't we been yet? We haven't looked in the kitchen, have we?'

He took the stairs two at a time. The kitchen had been recently modernized, and he groaned in disappointment. Nothing much to help him there, or in the attached scullery. But another room was half-hidden at the bottom of the staircase. The cellar. He backtracked to it.

Pushing the cracked, unpainted door open, he gazed inside. Stale air wafted out. Jack felt his mum arrive behind him, her breath warming his neck. A cooler draught seeped from somewhere nearby and, unseen, a black beetle scuttled between his feet. Sarah thought hard, nervous about where this was leading.

'It hasn't been used for years,' she said, getting in front of Jack in case he did something stupid like leap into the darkness.

'Hasn't it? You sure?'

'There's not even a working light down there. I checked last time I was here.'

A short flight of wooden steps led into the shadows. Jack couldn't quite make out the floor of the cellar, but something big was down there.

'Is that a chair?'

Peering closely, Sarah could see it as well – an ancient wooden rocking chair. It lay in the corner, one of its leg supports broken.

'Go on,' Jack said.

'What?'

'Go in, of course. Let's take a closer look. What are you waiting for?'

He started past her down the cellar steps, but she held him back.

'Uh-uh. Without a proper light, there's no way either of us is going down there. The steps are way too steep.'

'I'll be OK.'

'You'll break your neck.'

'Mum . . .'

'No!'

Jack craned his neck to look over her shoulder. Apart from the rocking chair, he was sure something else was sliding against the darkness. Then a patch of dust irritated his throat, and he had to reach into a pocket for another dose of his inhaler.

'He sees us!' Oliver shouted. 'I'm telling you! Look at him! He's staring right at us!'

The four ghost children gazed up from the dimness of the cellar floor. They'd followed Jack and his mother all around the house as best they could.

'Can he really see us?' Gwyneth gasped.

'No,' Ann said. 'I've told you before, no one can. Even if we'd like them to, living people never do.'

'But he keeps looking at us as if he *can* see us,' Charlie said.

Oliver floated up to the second step. 'Let's find out for sure.'

'What are you going to do?'

'I'm not just sitting down here in the dark. I think I'll go press myself right up against him. What do you reckon, Charlie? Face to face. Dead face to live face. See if he notices.'

Charlie stared at Oliver in awe as he floated rapidly to the top of the steps.

'Out you come. Right now.' Sarah turned Jack sharply round and closed the cellar door. 'There's way too much dust in there.'

'But –'

'No. I shouldn't have to remind you how careful you need to be until we can clean the place up, Jack, the way your asthma's been lately. Let's go.' She rested a hand against his chest, shaking her head. 'You're wheezing.'

'No, I'm not.' But he was – the musty air inflaming his lungs.

'Come on. Away from this dust pit.'

Ten minutes later they were both sitting at a small circular dining table in the kitchen, sipping instant coffee. One of Jack's hands rested on the oak table-top, his fingers making precise, delicate, exploratory movements. Was he really sensing people who had died in this house? No, Sarah thought. He was only *wishing* he had, just as he'd wished for so long for his dad to be back with them. She'd tried everything she could to help him overcome the loneliness following his father's death, shared her own grief with him, even tried counselling, but nothing seemed to reach him. How many times in the old house had she found Jack lying silently and wide-awake in some corner in the dark, with his dad's things gathered and heaped around him? He can't go through all that again, she thought. He can't. If he did, what would his mind be like at the end of it?

*

Seeing how nervous it made his mum, Jack didn't say anything more about dead people for the rest of the day. Instead, he helped her rearrange some of the furniture, and tried to put her at ease by talking about how he'd use the last couple of weeks left of school holidays to get out of the house and explore the area. Later, he changed the layout of his room about a bit, but really he was only biding his time, waiting for it to get dark. His gift for sensing people was always sharper at night, when household dust settled and everything was quiet.

Sarah followed him up to his room that evening. Once he was in his pyjamas, she tucked him in bed and kissed him lightly on the cheek. But she hesitated at the door.

'Are you sure about staying in this room? A dead person, Jack . . . it's no trouble moving you in with me for a while, you know.'

Jack shook his head.

'No way you're moving me out of here now, Mum.'

She nodded in resignation. 'On or off then?' she asked. She reached for the light switch, already knowing the answer she'd get.

Jack grinned. 'Off. Definitely off.'

As soon as she left, Jack checked his reliever inhaler was on the bedside table – just in case he needed it in the night – and nestled his head back on the pillows. That drop of blood! What on earth had been wrong with the girl? He wanted to sneak back to her room and spend all night by the window, finding out what he could, but he knew his mum would be on the lookout. If he behaved too weirdly, she'd make him leave. He couldn't let that happen, not yet. He had to know more.

For tonight he'd best stay in his bedroom. He had no problem with that. The room was intriguing enough all by itself. He was sure now that an old woman had died here, no more than a few months ago. The impressions of her were clearer in the dark, and he sat back and let them sink in. To Jack, there was nothing strange about what he was doing. He'd noticed that nearly everyone else avoided thinking or talking about death. They'd certainly never have slept in a bed where a person had just died. But why not? To Jack, that didn't make any sense. Living things died; that's what happened. At least this way, with his back up against the cotton sheets, his hands in contact with the pine frame, he could be closer to that dead person. What was so wrong with doing that? Weren't the dead worth remembering?

He sat up, re-positioned the picture of his dad so that he could see it clearly from the pillows, then lay still again. The curtains were slightly parted, letting in a splash of moonlight. It shone directly onto the wall behind his bed, picking out the sharp-edged shadow of a tree outside. The shadow ran back and forth across the ceiling like an animal, but Jack wasn't nervous. It was just a shadow. The woman who died here must have fallen asleep sometimes watching that shadow, he thought. For some reason the thought comforted him. He lay on top of the bedclothes, wide awake for hours, mildly frightened by what he'd experienced that day, but also excited by it, and enjoying the mixture of darkness and moonlight in the room.

He had nearly drifted off to sleep when he felt – a pressure. It came from the foot of the bed, as if someone had carefully sat down without wanting to disturb him. It was the slightest of pressures, almost nothing. Jack barely noticed it. And if he'd already fallen asleep perhaps he wouldn't have noticed the sigh either – a long sigh against his right ear, followed by a caress that reached across his shoulders and down onto his throat.

It was like a mother's caress, but it was not his mother.

Four

Attack

Jack screamed. A small, thin woman, face as pale as a white candle, was draped across his bed. Her arm was extended tenderly towards him. Her eyes, in the moonlight, were black as a bird's. Clearly startled that Jack could see her, she backed off. Her arms drifted, her body appearing to rise gradually up off the bed.

Jack lunged for the door. Even before he reached it, he was struggling to find air. By the next breath he was hyperventilating – inhaling too rapidly for enough oxygen to enter his lungs. He knew the pattern only too well: an asthma attack, brought on by shock.

Staggering to the door, he opened it, crawling into the corridor. 'Mum! MUM!' he rasped. The words barely emerged. He fumbled in his pyjama top pocket for his inhaler, but he'd left it on the table in his room. He couldn't go back. The woman was there.

As his air passages constricted, Jack felt the familiar tightening of his chest. His last bad asthma attack had been recent, which meant this one came on fast. He collapsed on the landing, howling with pain.

Stop it, he thought. Stop it. You have to stop it without the inhaler.

No longer pointlessly trying to shout, he went through his emergency action plan. It was something his mum had drilled into him since the first attack, when he was seven years old. *Relax. First, relax. Give your lungs a chance to recover naturally.* He heard her reassuring voice in his mind. If he'd been carrying his inhaler, he would have taken several carefully spaced metered dosages, and waited. He didn't have his inhaler, so he crouched down, to take the pressure off his chest, bent over and forced himself to breathe as steadily as possible. After half a minute the pain was worse, not better, and he realized with horror that it was already too late to stop the attack without medication.

Knowing that, Jack couldn't stay calm any more. He arched his back, and managed to throw his arm feebly against his mum's bedroom door. Sliding his knees forward, he glanced behind him.

There was no sign of the thin woman.

She had looked, he recalled, as if she was about to lean across the bed to kiss him. And it was the same woman he'd seen in the garden with the little girl. Definitely the same mother. Only this version was older, thinner, frailer.

'Jack?' Sarah stood blinking on the landing, pulling a chocolate-brown dressing gown around her. As soon as she saw his crouched-over shape she knew what was wrong, and ran back into her room, where she kept a reserve beta-agonist supplemental inhaler.

Seeing it, Jack reached up desperately.

She allowed him four inhalations. He wanted to take more, but too much of the drug would be dangerous.

'I'm here,' she said calmly. 'It's OK. Breathe. Come on. You know what to do. Follow my lead.' She got behind him, holding his head down at the proper angle, giving his air passages the room they needed to recover. 'Now,' she said, taking a single, deep, exaggerated, breath. Another breath. Another, all the while keeping her hands on Jack's shoulders, guiding and reassuring him with physical contact. Then she started to count. Methodically she counted out the precious breaths, one by one. Jack counted with her, and was finally allowed another burst from the inhaler. Not once did Sarah try to speak to him. She didn't ask him what had happened. That didn't matter right now. Speaking interrupted the rhythm. She focused only on his breathing. In and out. Gradually. With increasing slowness. To the sound of light rainfall falling outside, she silently held him and helped him breathe again.

Long before the attack was fully over, Jack managed a few strangled words.

'There . . . was . . . a woman.'

'A woman?'

'Next to me . . .' More agonized gasps. 'On . . . my bed.'

'Just now?' Sarah glanced in alarm towards his open bedroom door. She waited a few more seconds for Jack's breathing to come under control, never taking her eyes off the entrance. Then she cleared her throat and shouted a warning to whoever might be in there. A thief? When there was no reply, she tied her dressing gown firmly and looked inside. There was no one there. She searched Jack's bedroom thoroughly, followed by every room in the house. It was only when she was sure there was no intruder that she began to relax a little. By the time she returned to Jack, the beta-agonist inhaler had done its job, and his breathing was more normal.

'I've checked all over the house,' she told him. 'There's no one here.'

'What about the cellar?'

'I looked there, too. No one's broken in. The doors are locked. So are all the windows. Either locked, or painted shut. The windows big enough to climb in and out of are stuck tight. Whoever lived here before was obviously concerned about being burgled.'

'I'm not making this up, Mum.'

'I know. I'm not saying that.'

'You think I was dreaming?'

Had he been? It was possible. He breathed in deeply, gripping his mum's arm, still needing her support after the attack. 'Come on,' he said, forcing himself to go back into his bedroom. Sarah turned on the light. Jack stood near his bed – not too close.

'She was thinner than you,' he said. 'I mean really thin. Starving thin. And she was moving weirdly, almost above the bed. She looked . . . I don't know . . .' He shuddered, coughing twice.

Sarah made Jack go through his routine post-attack breathing exercises, waiting until his respiration was more composed. Then she gave him the test for his peak flow number, to measure how well his lungs were performing. The result was an orange warning light at first, but it turned to green – OK – within twenty minutes. When she was certain the asthma crisis was over, she helped him down the staircase into the lounge.

'I saw her before as well,' Jack said, feeling slightly foolish now about the way he'd reacted. 'It was the same woman who was with the little girl. Except this woman's face was white. No, wait. Maybe that was the effect of the moon …' Sarah sat beside him on the sofa. 'I know what you're thinking,' Jack said, making himself slow down. 'Here we are, in this old place, and me with my whole past thing going on, and I've worked myself into a state, dreamed up a dead person.' Her silence told him that was exactly what she thought. Well? Jack asked himself. Did you see a woman on the bed or not? Now, with the living-room lights blazing away, he wasn't quite so sure.

Relieved to see Jack's breathing back to something like normal, for the next hour or so Sarah stayed with him, assessing his mood. His voice was still hoarse – the after-effects of the asthma attack. She didn't mention the woman again. She didn't want that on his mind before he fell asleep if she could avoid it. Jack gradually came to accept that he could have dreamt her up, and traipsed back to his room.

'Why not come in with me for tonight?' Sarah suggested, seeing the way he hesitated to go inside. 'Just bring your mattress in, and –'

'No, it's OK.'

'I don't mind, Jack. In fact –'

'Honestly, Mum, I'm all right.' He grinned sheepishly. 'If I get scared, I'll watch TV or something. You go back to bed. I know where my medicine is. I'll be OK.'

Seeing that he was embarrassed, Sarah nodded, quickly kissed him on the cheek and left him alone. For the next few minutes she perched on the edge of her bed, simply listening to Jack breathe. She knew every tiny sound his throat made after an attack. She knew when to worry, when not to, when to phone 999. This was not one of those times. Even so, she eavesdropped for another hour or so, alert for any kind of unbalanced rhythm.

Was the whole fixation with his dad about to begin again? She faced the possibility, steeling herself for it. Let's just get through tonight, she thought, the same little mantra she'd told herself on all those other nights in the old house. One day at a time. Hearing nothing new from his room, she finally slipped into a fitful slumber.

Sleep wouldn't come for Jack. Finally he gave up trying, jumped out of bed and swished the curtains wide. It had stopped raining. Dark clouds raced across the sky, with the moon a dim halo behind them. He considered switching on his bedroom light, but didn't want to admit to himself that he needed to. He was uncomfortably aware that he was behaving like he had when his dad died, but this was different. He'd never actually *seen* his dad after he died. But he had seen the woman on the bed clearly. She'd scared him, too, and realizing that brought a thin smile to Jack's lips. Wasn't he supposed to be the one not afraid of dead people? Anyway, he'd dreamed her up, hadn't he? Maybe. Probably. But I did see her in the garden with the little girl, he thought. I didn't dream that up.

Jack made himself lie down on top of the sheets, shuddering as he remembered the light, feathery feel of the woman's hand. Then he sat up again, drawing the duvet over his knees. To distract himself, he read a little whenever the moon peeped out from behind the clouds, but left the light off. His breathing was still erratic. His nose remained blocked as well, and he kept sniffing. If his old attacks were anything to go by, the sniffing and occasional cough would last for days.

It was as he eased over onto his left side that Jack sensed something outside the room. As he turned, a white, elongated hand appeared under the crack at the bottom of his door. The hand reached under the door, as if fumbling for grip, and then pulled the rest of its body into the room.

Five

The Ghost Mother

Jack stifled a shriek. It was her – definitely the ghost woman again.

She rose rapidly up, drifting towards the ceiling, and it took all of Jack's self-control not to run. Drawing closer, she glided across the ceiling until she loomed, hovering, directly over him. Then she rotated and lowered herself as slowly as a mote of dust towards the bed.

Jack pulled in his legs, and she alighted next to him. If the ghost had made any kind of threatening gesture, Jack would have screamed. But she did not threaten him in any way. Her movements were serene, not hasty, the air currents in the room making her body flutter like a sheet in a languid breeze. Watching closely, Jack saw that she had to seize the mattress to keep herself from being blown away, she was so light.

'Well,' she whispered, 'an alarmed boy. Not alarmed by

33

me, I trust?' She smiled uneasily. Her teeth were crooked, a few discoloured, one entirely black.

Jack jerked his knees up, clutching the sheets around him.

It was recognizably the mother of the little girl he'd seen in the old garden, but how she'd changed: so much thinner, more haggard. A plain crêpe dress, down to her ankles, hugged her bony frame, and it was utterly black, as if she was *still* in mourning. There was something disturbing about the dress as well: it was ripped at the neck, torn violently open. Moonlight spilled across her throat.

But one thing gave Jack a little more courage. She was clearly scared. She looked as scared of seeing him as he was of her. A great shiver passed through her body. Seeing it unfroze Jack's voice enough to ask a question.

'Are you . . . are you cold?'

'I do not feel the cold,' she answered. 'In any case, your room is far warmer than mine ever was, Jack.'

'You know my name?'

The ghost woman smiled. 'Your mother says it tenderly and often enough.'

Her voice was gentle, reassuring.

Little by little she circled his bed, never quite touching the ground. Her light body was affected in bizarre ways by the slight breezes in the room. Her head, caught in a current of air from the window, blew backward, her hair flying straight out, the neck muscles forcefully straining. At the same time, the rest of her body was caught in a down-draught descending from the ceiling. No part of her was ever quite still. It was dizzying to watch her for long.

'I am sorry I affrighted you earlier,' she said. 'I did not mean for that to happen. But you also affrighted me. I never had a son, you know, though I often wished for one of my own. May I?'

Jack realized that she wanted to touch his face.

He hesitated, then said yes.

She bent across and ran her fingers through his hair. Her touch, Jack was grateful to find, was warm, and so light that he could barely feel it. Her fingertips strayed onto his cheek and she smiled timidly. A breeze lifted the smile, pulling it upward before letting it go again.

'Who are you?' Jack murmured.

'Oh, but who are you?' she asked him back. 'There has never been a one entering this house who could see me. More remarkable than a ghost: what nature of thing are you, Jack, that you can see and converse with the dead?'

She sat tensely above the sheets, passing his hair gently between her thumb and forefinger. Then she dropped her head closer to his, and Jack flinched as her disarrayed black locks spilled across his face.

'Oh, yes,' she whispered, looking him over thoroughly. 'I think my beloved daughter Isabella would have liked you . . .'

Jack should have been able to feel her breath this close to him, but there was no breath. No odours from her, either. No smells at all.

'Isabella?' Jack whispered. 'Were you her mother?'

'Mother?' She seemed to turn that around in her mind. 'Yes, I suppose. If a ghost can still call itself such a thing, I am, or was, though there is no one who calls me by that name now. A *Ghost Mother*. Yes, I like the sound of that. I . . .

can be your Ghost Mother, perhaps. Would you like one of those?'

Jack wasn't quite sure what to reply.

'What was . . . is your name?' he asked.

'My name?' The Ghost Mother didn't appear to be interested in this question, so Jack asked another.

'Are you alone here?'

'Indeed, I am nothing but an old dead mother, without a child these many past years.' The Ghost Mother plucked at her lower lip. 'But here we are, talking like fast friends, when I have not yet introduced you to my beloved! Please forgive me.' She sighed, her expression suddenly emotional.

'I am asking you to imagine a girl, Jack. She was twelve years old when Death took her from me. Is that your age, too?' Jack nodded and the Ghost Mother smiled. 'Her name was Isabella Kate Rosewood, and she was a daughter of mine once upon a time, and a good one. I will not elevate her in your eyes, for I do not believe that one child should be elevated above any other. In any case, she left us more than a century and a half past, since which time I have been alone in the world, with only memories of her to keep me comfort. Can I tell you some of them, Jack? Do you wish to hear more about her?'

Jack swallowed. He could tell how much the Ghost Mother wanted to go on.

'I'd . . . yes . . . like to hear more,' he said.

The Ghost Mother put her hand on her heart. Jack could see her concentrating furiously.

'I . . . I cannot recall everything, but . . .' She stopped, licked her lips. 'I recall that . . .' She clenched her fists, her voice suddenly trapped in her throat. Jack wanted to help her. At first he thought she was having difficulty because she was overwhelmed with emotion. Gradually he saw it was because she could not remember.

She screamed then, so suddenly that Jack jerked back. Her hands covered her face. Between fingers clenched over her mouth, she rasped, 'A terrible time Isabella had of it in that room, Jack! Long I prayed that my love would be enough, for the horror of her affliction to take me instead, but it would not. Love, and a dear heart? What are those compared with the Captain of Death? He took my husband and my daughter. He takes what he will. And all the hope and tears in the world cannot bring back those we cherish.'

The Ghost Mother gripped the frame of the bed, to steady herself.

Jack instinctively reached out his hand to her, thinking of his own dad. Hesitantly, he asked, 'How did they die?'

'Consumption.' She shot out a bitter laugh. 'The beautiful disease, I have heard it called. And for a time the victims do have a rosy hue, the cheeks gleam prettily; a fever gilds the skin, makes it shine! Isabella had that, too, but in the end the only thing left is the cough. You should have seen her, Jack, like an angel the fierce way she struggled to stay alive. She never gave in to it. Never.'

The Ghost Mother bowed her head. 'But sometimes I wished she *would* give in. That she might have died sooner, faster, to lessen her suffering. Was that wrong of me?'

Jack had no idea what to say. He sat there, only wanting to comfort the Ghost Mother.

'Winter was worst,' she said. 'When we could afford

37

wood or furze, we'd sometimes sit by the hearth all day as a treat, and have a warm, just as you and your own mother did this afternoon. But after my husband passed away, I could not look after an invalid daughter and a farm as well, and things went badly for us. I was forced to sell the land and take whatever work I could get. Apprenticed once to a seamstress, I knew darning and patching and a maid's tasks well enough. I'd run errands, too, skivvy, mend shoes, man's work they say, but I took it, whatever was offered, and, well . . .' She spread her pale hands. 'All of that made no difference in the end, did it? No amount of hard work or love can stop the Captain taking what he will.'

The Ghost Mother slumped on the bed, her hair drifting vertically on a breeze. 'I am sorry,' she murmured. 'As a first conversation between strangers, these are cheerless words. I will take my leave now. But –' she glanced at Jack with sudden desperation and hope '– may I have your permission for a second visit? Will you keep an old dead Ghost Mother company for a while?'

'Yes,' Jack said.

'In that case I will trouble you no further tonight.'

'Don't go yet,' he said. 'Tell me . . . please tell me one thing.'

'One thing? Very well. I might tell you one thing.'

'Did you die here, in this house?'

'I did,' she replied without hesitation.

'How did you die?'

'That is two questions, Jack.'

'Please answer.'

'I cannot bear to tell you that yet. I may never be able

to.' She stared at him thoughtfully. 'I have one request of my own to beg of you, Jack. It is only a small matter. I ask that you do not tell your mother about me. She will only think you are lying, and try to take you away. I do not want that to happen, so soon after meeting you. Will you keep your silence?'

Jack slowly nodded, and the Ghost Mother smiled, properly relaxing for the first time.

'In that case, good night, Jack. Good night, lovely boy.'

She departed without a backward glance, sliding noiselessly under the door.

After she left, Jack lay on his bed, staring up at the ceiling. The way the Ghost Mother had moved! He was frightened, exhilarated, full of sadness for her, fascinated by her. A ghost in the house! The idea thrilled him. She thrilled him. And she would visit again. What could have happened that was so awful she couldn't talk about it? Well, he would ask more about that next time he saw her . . .

Closing his eyes, Jack tried to imagine what it might be like to spend all that time in the house without ever talking to anyone. One hundred and fifty years! Wouldn't you go mad? A Ghost Mother, he thought. Two mothers under one roof. One alive, one dead.

Jack's last thoughts before he fell asleep, however, had nothing to do with mothers. At first he decided he must be dreaming about Isabella, because it was a girl's voice he was hearing. But he soon realized that it was a song. A kind of comfort song. Like a lullaby from an older child to soothe a younger one. And it made no sense to him at all.

When children are playing alone on the green,
In comes the playmate that never was seen.
When children are happy and lonely and good,
The Friend of the children comes out of the wood.

Deep in the darkness of the house, Ann finished singing the strange verse Gwyneth had always liked so much and looked down at her small, sleeping face. It was good that Gwyneth slept. Now that the Ghost Mother was awake, there would be little sleep in the days to come for any of them.

Charlie floated near Ann, thinking about his own death. Seeing Sarah's concern over Jack had stirred up all sorts of memories for him again, including the way his mother had held his hand at the end of his life – that last touch at the hospital. For the first time in as long as he could remember, Charlie wondered if she might still be alive. He'd only been trapped in the house for thirty-five years. It was possible.

He gave Ann a wistful half glance, and she smiled reassuringly back.

Oliver grunted, and put his ear to the scullery door, impatient to find out what was going on in the rest of the house. Normally, when she woke, the Ghost Mother came straight to find the ghost children. What was keeping her this time?

'I'm off to see what she's up to,' he told Ann.

'No,' she answered. 'You stay here. I'll go.'

Oliver stared at her curiously. Each time the Ghost Mother woke, Ann was always anxious to see her before the rest of them. Oliver wasn't sure why, but he knew it was dangerous. He could tell that because Ann usually returned so weak that she could barely speak.

'Not this time,' Oliver said. 'Anyway, it's been a while since she chased me. I need the practice.'

Before the others could object, he slipped out of the scullery, drifted along the corridor and found a curl of dry air to glide him up into the warmth of the upper house.

Six

The Death Room

When Jack woke next morning the memory of his conversation with the Ghost Mother was still fresh in his mind. He wanted to go straight downstairs and tell his mum, then remembered his promise.

Rolling out of bed, he rubbed his head, still feeling a bit woozy – the usual light-headedness he always experienced after an asthma attack. He took his time getting dressed, and inhaled the modified dosage of anti-inflammatory drugs his mum had made up for him last night. Entering the kitchen, he found her already sitting at the dining table, sipping a cappuccino. Coffee was all she ever had for breakfast.

'Sleep all right?' she asked, eyeing him over the rim of her cup.

'Like a baby,' Jack replied, a bit too quickly.

'Mm.' Sarah popped four slices of bread in the toaster.

While she waited for the slices to burn — Jack preferred them blackened at the edges — she poured him out some tea, wincing as Jack ladled in three heaped spoonfuls of sugar.

'I've phoned the doctor,' she said. 'He's coming tomorrow morning. Nothing to worry about. Only a check-up to make sure you're all right after last night. Better stay inside today, though, just to be safe. Take it easy and keep your medication handy. OK?'

Jack nodded, desperate to talk about the Ghost Mother. She glanced sidelong at him, able to tell at once that he was hiding something.

'So,' she said, watching him closely, 'have you thought any more about what happened last night?'

'What do you mean?'

'I mean the woman, of course.'

Jack squirmed. 'No, must've just dreamed her. I was asleep, and —'

'You don't really believe that, do you?'

Jack bit his lip and half turned away. Something about the way he did it made Sarah realize that the rest of the night had not been uneventful.

'Jack, tell me.'

'No, I . . .'

But he knew she'd never stop now until she dragged it out of him, so he did: about Isabella, about the Ghost Mother, everything. And it was a mistake. He knew almost immediately that she didn't believe one word. And why should she? Even he could hardly believe his own story, it sounded so weird. He couldn't stop his fingers fluttering against the wall next him as he told her, either, the same

43

nervous trait he'd shown over and over in the days after his dad died.

Sarah's heart sank. So that's why you wanted to come to this old house so much, she thought. You hoped being around even older things might give you a different way to bring your dad back again, didn't you? It's all about him. It's *still* all about him. We haven't got away at all.

While Jack continued to talk, at some point she stopped listening altogether, and said softly, 'Was anyone else in the room with the Ghost Mother, Jack?'

'No. Why should there have been?' Jack shrugged the remark aside. 'She was . . . she was . . . just talking and touching me gently on the throat and face. Like this.' He showed her, brushing his skin. 'I was scared, but it was all right. It didn't hurt. I didn't mind. I freaked out that first time I saw her, but I shouldn't have. I realize that now. She wasn't trying to harm me.'

Sarah gazed at him intently, saying nothing.

'Her touch was light,' Jack said, 'but it was still like this.' He took his mum's hand and drew it against his neck. 'It wasn't cold.' He smiled.

Sarah licked her dry lips. 'You liked that? A dead person touching you? Was anyone with the woman, Jack?' Very quietly.

'No.'

'Are you sure? Are you sure your dad wasn't there as well?'

'What?'

'Or somewhere nearby? Isn't that what you were thinking about or hoping before you went to sleep? That you'd be able to find him again? That the house being so

44

old, he might come here, or something like that?'

Jack stepped back, suddenly realizing what she meant.

'No, Mum. Listen to me! Dad wasn't with her. This has got nothing to do with Dad. Nothing.' He stared her out. 'Mum, I wasn't even thinking about him. But I *did* see the woman. She kept drifting up off the bed, like this . . .' He demonstrated, his arms rising slightly. 'But you know something weird? She's a ghost, but I'm not afraid of her, not really. If you'd heard the way she talked about Isabella, you wouldn't be scared of her, either. She's alone, Mum. She's been alone for ages.'

Sarah, with no idea how to deal with this yet, let the conversation end. Jack could tell she didn't believe him, and the more he tried to persuade her the less she listened, fixing him with a confused stare. He finally left her standing in the kitchen, the coffee cup shaking slightly in her hand, and returned in frustration to his own room.

Jack lay on his bed, playing a PC game, but secretly keeping a close lookout for the Ghost Mother. How could he find her again? Perhaps he didn't need to. If he was alone, maybe she'd come to *him*, like the first time. A haunting! he thought. That's what this is like. What did you do to encourage ghosts to haunt you? Did they need encouragement?

First Jack shut his door, closed the curtains and simply waited. When that didn't work, he lay down on the bed in the same position as before, anticipating the feel of her hand on his face. But the Ghost Mother surprised him. She didn't sneak in under the door this time. Instead, she lifted a hand out from underneath him, beneath the pillow on

45

which his head rested. As both her arms emerged, swaying over his head, Jack realized that he must have been lying partially against her, half inside her arms, for a long time without realizing it. It was only when he twisted to look down at her that she broke the embrace.

'Good morrow, Jack,' she said, thrusting herself into the room. 'I trust you are well rested?'

Her shape condensed against a wall briefly, then rebounded off it towards him again.

Jack said nothing, still recovering from the thought of being furtively encircled in her arms. He didn't like that, and it was also unnerving to watch her shape flowing in and out of the shadows of the room. A quietly confident smile broke over her face. She settled once more on the edge of his bed, grinning at him with her uneven teeth.

'I notice that you told your mother all about me.'

'I'm sorry. I didn't mean –'

'It does not matter,' the Ghost Mother said dismissively. 'I forgive you. Let us talk no further of her. I prefer to talk about *us*.' She gave a little sigh. 'It is good to imagine being of the living world once more, Jack. A mother talking to her son. I like it, even if it is only make-believing.'

She seemed much more self-assured today, though every small gesture still showed Jack how desperate she was for him to like her.

'Isabella,' he said. 'I –'

'You want to know more about her?'

'Yes.'

'Then do you believe in miracles, Jack?' She folded her arms across her chest, anger edging her voice. 'For I was offered them aplenty. If I could show you all the quack

46

cures I purchased to cure Isabella's consumption! Marvels, we were promised, if I paid enough. Once, God forgive me, I even rubbed salt in Isabella's gums, for that was said to be a restorative.' The Ghost Mother's neck drifted slightly towards Jack, caught in a breeze flowing under the door. 'Nothing worked. But at least Isabella never saw my tears. I wept them bitterly enough when that first dash of blood sprang forth out of her lovely mouth, but kept them from her sight thereafter.'

Jack told her what he'd seen when he felt the window frame and floor in Isabella's room.

'Touch, then?' the Ghost Mother mused. 'Memories springing from touch?' Her hand fluttered towards Jack for support, and he took it, gently at first, interlinking each of her wispy, insubstantial fingers in his own.

'You want to know more?' she asked, her expression suddenly more calculating. 'Oh, I think you should.'

Her grip tightened.

'What's going on?' Jack said.

She did not reply. She merely stared at him, licking her lips in concentration. She held his hand – seeking the memory she wanted Jack to see.

'Stop it,' Jack whispered.

'You want to understand what happened, don't you?'

'Yes . . . but . . .'

'But you're afraid, Jack? Is that what you're trying to say? Well, no matter. So was I. Fear and death: good friends they are. But to know Isabella you must see how the horror ended, as well as how it began.'

'Don't,' Jack said. 'Please . . .' He stared at the Ghost Mother, almost yanked his hand away, but didn't, kept it there, let her fingers envelop his.

'Do not be frightened,' she said. 'You want to understand, don't you? To do that you must stare our good friend the Captain in the face.'

A death room. It was many years later, and the carefree young Isabella was gone. The Isabella Jack saw now was close to his own age, closer still to her last breath. She sat in her old bedroom, looking out onto the garden. Four pillows propped her up on a wooden rocking chair, and she was like an emaciated doll, hunched up and almost lost amongst them. There was a permanent breathlessness to her now, a coarse crackle that never left her throat. Sweat drenched her face and clothes, and Jack saw that she barely had the strength left to even lever up her neck.

Her lips were unnaturally full and red, her eyes bruised, her face appallingly gaunt. But it was the way Isabella breathed that was the most terrifying thing. Every breath came into her light and horribly fast – like someone frantically catching their wind after a long run.

Her final breaths were like this, Jack realized. Snatched desperately from the air. This is what she looked like just before she died.

As he watched, Isabella cleared her throat several times, trying to free it so that she could breathe more easily, but a cough interrupted her. It was a startling cough, reminding Jack of the one when she was a little girl, but much worse, racking her whole body like a branch in the wind. Jack had coughed many times when his asthma was bad, but never like this. He knew a cough half as severe would have sent him crawling to his mum's room for help. Isabella, however, just clenched her fists, dealing with it as if she had done so many times before.

It was cold outside, the sky heavy with a winter rain that had not yet begun to fall. The Ghost Mother, looking thin and frail herself, entered the room and knelt beside Isabella, draping a shawl across her feet. Isabella thanked her, then gazed disconsolately out of the window. Her hand rested limply on the terrier's head. He was an older dog now, grey around his muzzle and legs. 'Sam,' she murmured. 'Sam, Sam.'

Outside, the first drops of rain fell and Isabella was carried by her mother from the chair to the iron bedstead. A white linen nightgown waited there, neatly folded. There were no mirrors in the room, but there were a few cut winter flowers. Some food lay untouched on the floor. Closer still, there was a pitcher and bowl.

'Here, drink this.'

Her mother held a tumbler of water to Isabella's lips. Isabella drank in small, jerky sips, like a bird drinking. When she put out a hand to hold the tumbler herself, the weight of it seemed to pull her. She dropped it with a clatter onto the tray, and laughed breathlessly.

The rain fell more heavily, big drops raking the house. Without moving her head, Isabella watched a flight of wood pigeons sweep past the window.

'Rain, rain, go away,' she murmured.

'Spring will soon be here,' her mother said. 'Not long now, not long at all.'

'I know.'

But Isabella had a resigned look, as if she had only said it for her mother's sake. She closed her eyes and lifted her

49

hand. Her mother caught it, pressed the palm against her lips and drew Isabella towards her.

The Ghost Mother slowly released her grip. For a while she and Jack sat together in silence in the bedroom, the Ghost Mother quietly weeping, but also glancing up sharply now and again from her lowered eyes to see how Jack was taking it all.

Jack had no idea what to say or think. He was entirely lost in the Ghost Mother's despair. But then something new happened that made him gasp. It was his gift, reaching out. It wasn't the same as before, feeding itself on a few paltry scraps of memories embedded in old furniture. It had been quickened, deepened, by whatever the Ghost Mother had done to him. His dad's death, the more recent death of the old woman in the house, Isabella's window, and now this, especially this, had awakened it beyond anything he'd known before.

Jack reeled, his head spinning.

There were more ghosts in this house.

He sensed them – only vaguely, but he knew they were there. The Ghost Mother wasn't the only spirit still living here. She was merely the strongest, the most visible.

Children, he realized. Somewhere in the house, huddled together. No. Wait. One was on the move – a single ghost meandering towards his bedroom, whisked on a breeze from downstairs. It had to be another ghost. No ordinary child could move like that.

The Ghost Mother hadn't mentioned them. Why? Wasn't she aware of them? If not, should he tell her?

'What is it, Jack?'

'This isn't right,' he said, feeling his way towards the truth. 'Somehow it isn't. You shouldn't be here at all, should you? I've never found anyone's spirit left behind in a house before. You're . . . you're meant to have passed on somewhere else, aren't you? Why are you stuck in this house?'

'I . . .' The Ghost Mother gazed away, her body drifting towards the window.

Jack glanced at her sharply.

'Did any other children die here apart from Isabella?' he demanded.

'Other children?'

'There are more ghosts here.'

'More?' The Ghost Mother tried to look surprised, but Jack could tell at once she was lying.

'So you *do* know about the children!'

She appraised him a moment, as if deciding how much to reveal.

'You seem to have a gift for finding the dead, Jack. I wonder where it will lead you?' She ran her hands through her hair, and something about the calculating way she appraised him suddenly made Jack nervous. For the first time he became conscious that he was alone with her, and how far away his mum was.

'One of the ghost children is heading towards us,' he said.

'They have . . . they have been in the house for many years,' she answered reluctantly, waving her arms as if to dismiss them.

'Tell me more,' Jack insisted.

'You don't need to know about them. Better you don't.

51

Little of their energy is left, thankfully.'

'What do you mean?'

'As spirits we are constantly fading, Jack, the longer we remain.'

'But *you're* not fading.'

'I am – only more slowly. Pay no attention to them, Jack. Ignore them. They are mere wisps.' The Ghost Mother's voice was choked with irritation. 'They are, in fact, spiteful and vindictive, young but far from innocent. And not to be trusted, not one word. I had hoped to shield you from them if I could. No doubt they will try to spout their lies at you.'

'Lies about what?'

'Why, about me, of course.' The Ghost Mother drifted closer to Jack, deeply agitated. 'Will you ignore them if they attempt to speak with you? I do not wish to share you, Jack, with blackened souls such as theirs. I love you too much already for that.'

Love? The word threw him totally.

'Forgive me,' she recovered at once. 'I mean, of course, the idea of having a son after all these years. That is what I love. Perhaps . . . perhaps, if you permit it, I really can be a kind of second mother to you. We can pretend. I will call you son, and you will call me Mother. Is that too much to ask?'

Jack could see how much she wanted it. He nodded uncertainly.

'Good,' she said. 'You will not tell Sarah any more about me, I hope? Mothers are passionate, jealous creatures. She might not like having a second mother in the house. She will make you leave. We don't want that, do we?' He could see her lips trembling, obviously trying to hold back deeper feelings, but unable to.

'Call me Mother,' she burst out. 'Will you . . . will you do that?'

'What?'

'Call me Mother.'

'Mother,' Jack whispered, his throat dry.

'Say it again.'

'Mother.'

'Once more.'

'Mother.'

'Thank you.' She bent down to kiss him. Jack shrank back a little. He didn't want her kissing him again. He was suddenly afraid of her touch.

'This is how Sarah kisses you, isn't it?' she said. 'On the cheek, or forehead. I have watched her. So our greeting and leave-taking will be different. I will kiss your neck. That will be our way.' She smiled. 'And if you will give me a chance,' she went on brightly, 'I believe that I may in time become as good a mother to you as Sarah has ever been. Who knows, a better one, perhaps? One you prefer. Do you think that is possible? Do you think I could replace your mother?'

The thought repelled Jack. As he struggled even to take it in, the Ghost Mother put her fingers to his lips.

'No, no, I see it is too soon to ask that. I understand. I should not have mentioned it. Naturally your loyalties are to your own mother, as any good son's ought to be. That itself warms me to you. It is how I would want my own son to be. I —'

She stopped, her eyes glinting coldly.

Jack knew why. One of the other ghosts was now in the room with them. Jack couldn't see whoever it was, but he knew the child was nearby.

The Ghost Mother glanced at Jack, obviously hoping that he couldn't detect anything. When she saw he could, a flash of anger crossed her face, and she shouted to the room at large, 'Don't you dare, Oliver! Stay back! Stay away!'

'Oliver?' Jack whispered. 'A boy?'

He sensed the ghost child better now that he was close: yes, definitely a boy – in the room, at the entrance, defiant.

'Stay here, Jack, I beg you!' the Ghost Mother implored him. 'It is dangerous to follow. He will hurt you!'

With a final warning look, she floated rapidly towards the door.

Seven

Flight

Oliver fled. Normally he'd have tried to hide from the Ghost Mother in a crack or shadow, but she was so close that it was too late to hide.

Slipping under Jack's door, he floated onto the landing, anxiously searching for a descending air flow. There was none. Oliver found himself rising, caught in a drift of warm air rushing up the staircase. The Ghost Mother was behind him, trapped in the same air current. Her hair spilled forward over her face in long sinuous waves.

'For interfering, I'm going to punish you, Oliver,' she told him. 'Unless you give in to me now. Unless you do it voluntarily.'

The updraught jammed Oliver up against the landing ceiling. When he couldn't find a cross-breeze to escape on, he had no choice except to wait for the Ghost Mother. Conserving his energy, he planted his feet firmly on the plaster, ready to push off.

Never before had the Ghost Mother been so close to catching Oliver. For years she'd ridden the breezes of the house after him, hoping for a chance like this. Concentrating, she moderated her speed, checked her trajectory, and took dead aim for him. No deviation. No allowing perturbations of the updraught to deflect her. Oliver had avoided her all too often by exploiting such tiny miscalculations on her part.

'There's no escape this time,' she called up to him. 'I've learned a lot by studying you, Oliver. Especially the way you cup your hands to use the breezes. You shouldn't have shown me that.'

Oliver had never attempted such a dangerous manoeuvre as he did now, but he had no choice. Waiting until the Ghost Mother was almost upon him, he kicked hard off the ceiling and jack-knifed under her. Barely scraping past her clutching arms, he grasped her legs and pulled hard, thrusting himself downward.

It gave him just enough momentum to overcome the updraught.

The Ghost Mother searched frantically for a sinking wisp of air, found one near the wall, and followed him. Oliver headed for the cellar. It was the deepest part of the house. If he could reach it first, there might be a place to hide. The chase was close, but part of that was Oliver deliberately hanging back. At the last second he surprised the Ghost Mother. Just as he entered the cellar, letting her almost catch him, he seized the door frame and reversed direction – ascending the staircase again.

The Ghost Mother hadn't expected that. Unable to

snatch Oliver in time, she sailed into the partially open doorway, and once within the cellar continued to gradually plummet, sinking into the darkness.

Oliver swore cheerfully at her over his shoulder, then rode the warm updraught all the way into Isabella's old room. The rest of the ghost children were waiting for him there.

'You did it!' Charlie cried. 'You got away!'

Oliver smirked. 'Never mind that, Charlie boy. Wait till you hear what our new boy Jack's been up to. Listen: he *saw* old Weepy! He saw her and then, get this, he *talked* to her! He sat up in bed, duvet tucked up over his knees, chatting away as if he talked to dead people like her all the time!'

There was stunned silence, while the others took this in.

'Wasn't he scared?' Gwyneth asked at last.

'Not a bit!' Oliver said. 'He doesn't know her like we do. He let her do whatever she liked. Even let her do this!'

Gwyneth shrank back as Oliver kissed her neck.

Ann tried to take all this in. Impossible: a living boy who could see a ghost! She could only imagine the lengths the Ghost Mother would go to have him to herself.

'What was her reaction?' she asked.

'Oh, she absolutely loved it, of course!' Oliver said. 'In her element, wasn't she? Jack's everything she's ever wanted, and all the usual stuff came out, her crying her eyes out, how she didn't like to compare any child to another, but oh let me tell you about my sweet darling Isabella! Oh yes, old Weepy loved it all right. A living child who can see her. Someone able to hold her dead old hand

hand without feeling sick! She was practically begging Jack to be her son from the second he opened his mouth.'

'Could Jack see you?'

'I'm sure he did, absolutely certain.' Oliver grinned at Charlie, still elated by the chase. 'We'd better decide quick what we're going to do. Weepy'll soon get out of the cellar, and she's not exactly going to be happy if she finds any of us right now. We've spoiled her day. She wanted nice Jack all to herself.'

Charlie floated closer to Oliver. 'Maybe,' he said, 'maybe . . . she'll leave us alone now.'

'What do you mean?'

'You know, if she's got Jack. If we let her have him. If she's got a live boy, she won't hurt us for a while. She won't . . . won't feed on us.'

Charlie's words affected them all. Oliver was the only one of the children who hadn't been caught in recent years by the Ghost Mother. Each of the others had vivid memories of being cornered, and the feeling as the Ghost Mother clamped her face onto theirs — followed by the usual screaming. It was the way she nourished herself, kept her spirit strong.

'Do you think you could get a message to Jack?' Ann asked Oliver.

'What kind of message?'

'One telling him how much danger he's in. To get out of the house.'

'But Jack's *alive*. He's not like us, Ann. How can she hurt him?'

'She'll find a way,' Ann said. 'It's just a matter of time.'

'But she likes him!'

Ann smiled darkly. 'Oh yes. She likes him now. And she'll be nice enough until Jack rejects her. Then she'll go berserk, just like with us. Jack's flesh and blood, so she might not be able to harm him, but when he doesn't do what she wants, she'll try. You know that. We've got to get him out of here.'

'No!' Charlie blurted. 'Don't go, Oliver. She'll *really* be after you now! It's dangerous leaving messages.'

Gwyneth tapped Ann's shoulder. 'If Jack can see us, can we play with him?'

Ann sighed. It would certainly have been nice to have had a conversation with Jack. Someone new. And a chance at last of contact with the world outside as well. It was deeply tempting. But every moment Jack was exposed to the Ghost Mother, they risked something appalling happening.

'I'll get the message to him,' Oliver said.

'She'll be waiting for you!' Charlie wailed.

'So what? She's always waiting for me somewhere.'

'Charlie's right,' Ann said. 'You'll have to be especially careful this time, Oliver. And it's not going to be easy leaving a message, either. It's got to be a message *not* seen by her, or she'll punish us. Even if she can't catch you, you know what she'll do to the rest of us.'

Oliver nodded sombrely. 'She won't know I was there. I'll make sure.'

'How?'

'I don't know yet! Depends on the situation.' He made a move to leave, but Charlie held his arm.

'Surprised you're making such a fuss,' Oliver said, removing it gently. 'Old Weepy's not caught me in years.

She's probably down there in the cellar right now, scared stiff, wetting her old pants at the thought I might get to Jack first. Either that, or she's in his room, the fraud, perched on his bed, waiting to chat to him like she's his real mummy. Don't worry, I'll be ready for her, wherever she is.'

'Just tell Jack to get out,' Ann said firmly. 'Just tell him that.'

Oliver grinned. 'A message that'll frighten him to death, you mean?'

'Yes.'

'Something that'll make him grab his mum's hand straight away and run off screaming into the night? That the sort of thing you've got in mind?'

'Yes.'

'All right. Where will you be after I tell him?'

Ann thought about that. 'In the scullery, if we can get there without being seen. If she comes after us we'll scatter, and I'll meet you wherever I can.'

'Better hope I'm not spotted talking to Jack,' he whispered in her ear. 'If I am, Weepy won't rest till she gets a bit of revenge. And she'll come straight for *you*, Ann, like she always does.'

'Don't worry about me,' Ann said. 'I can take care of myself, if I have to. Just be careful. Don't take any stupid risks.'

Oliver gave her a quick smile, winked at Charlie and skimmed under the door.

Eight

The Rocking Chair

Jack sat back on his bed, still stunned by the explosive surge of anger from the Ghost Mother. The ghost children were mischievous, apparently. They were liars, dangerous, definitely not to be trusted. Was that true? He wished now he'd ignored the Ghost Mother's warning, and followed the boy. By the time he did start searching, all the ghosts, including the mother, seemed to have gone into hiding.

What was going on in this house? Jack shook his head, wondering if there was a way he could use his gift to get to the bottom of the mystery. Well, perhaps there was. Taking a quick squirt from his inhaler, he hurried down the staircase. His mum was in the kitchen, the radio on, preparing lunch. Jack eased the cellar door open as quietly as possible. At first all he could see was darkness. Then the outline of the old rocking chair filtered through the shadows. There you are, Jack thought. Filthy and forgotten. But not by me. Let's see what you've got to say for yourself. Taking a relatively clean breath of air from outside the cellar, he trod carefully down the steps.

The Ghost Mother watched Jack. Crouched in the deepest shadow of the cellar, where he could not see her, she observed him fondly. She preferred it this way, staring at him without him knowing, free to look at his every move without him becoming self-conscious about being watched. As Jack descended the steps, she feasted her eyes on the arch of his neck – a neck he had so recently allowed her to kiss.

Everything about Jack consumed and excited her. A live boy to spend time with at last! So much better than the ghost children. They never allowed themselves to be kissed by her the way Jack had. And hadn't she already given him the perfect memory to fully open up his heart to her – a dying Isabella? Jack already felt sorry for her, she was certain of that. Sympathy would do for now, until she could find a way to deepen his affection.

The Ghost Mother suppressed a sigh. Given the chance, she would happily have stayed no more than inches from Jack's face, following him everywhere. But one thing bothered her. As Jack fumbled around the cellar floor, she found it odd that he should take such an interest in Isabella's old chair. That disturbed her. She didn't like him touching it.

Jack hauled the rocking chair out of the cellar as quietly as he could, and carried it up to Isabella's old bedroom.

Wheezing and suppressing a cough, he positioned it near the window. There, he thought, making a final adjustment of the angle. Right here – overlooking the garden, able to look out onto the flowers. That's the way you preferred the chair, wasn't it?

He ran his palm over one of the wooden arms. Instantly the shape of Isabella's ever-weakening hand tingled under his. A painfully thin hand. She had weighed virtually nothing by the end. Thinking back to the memory the Ghost Mother gave him, he remembered how easy it had been for Isabella to be lifted from the chair onto the iron bed in her final days.

Jack tiptoed around the chair, still not quite ready to sit in it, nervous about what he might discover. Outside, a cloud blew across the sun.

'Lunch in five minutes!' Sarah's voice yelled up the stairs.

'OK!' Jack shouted back.

The rocking chair had a broken strut. The joints were infested with woodworm.

Never mind, Jack thought, easing himself down into the seat.

The second he did so the Ghost Mother rose up next to his face. Jack had never seen anything like her expression before: a gaze full of possessive loathing, like an angel of vengeance.

'Get out!' she wailed. 'Out of her chair! Get out! Get out!'

Shocked, Jack fell from the seat to the floor.

'I . . .' He couldn't talk. His chest was instantly tight, going into spasm. Quickly reaching into his jeans, he took two squirts from his reliever inhaler, then turned back to the Ghost Mother.

She floated above the chair, guarding it, her mouth twitching with anger.

'Why did you sit there?' she shrieked. 'How could you? It was Isabella's alone, not yours! Is this the gratitude I deserve for becoming a mother again, and pretending I have a son? Is this the thanklessness I deserve after unburdening my heart to you?'

Jack tried to explain, to apologize, since that's what she wanted, but he couldn't catch his breath. In any case, the Ghost Mother wasn't listening. She drifted in agitation around the room, tearing at her own hair, repeatedly striking her chest. Eventually she composed herself and settled near Jack.

He edged away from her, frightened of what she might do next.

'I didn't mean,' he began, '. . . didn't mean to . . .'

'Jack!' Sarah shouted up. 'Where are you? Downstairs now! Food's ready!'

Jack didn't dare take his eyes off the Ghost Mother.

She sat immobile for a moment, the hatred draining from her face. Then she forced out a smile. After all the fury, the smile alarmed him more than anything else she might have done.

'Help me, Jack,' she said softly. 'Will you help me?'

'Of . . . course,' Jack replied, anxious to pacify her. 'What do you want me to do?'

'Nothing much. Go to your room and fetch a pillow. That is all.'

'Why?'

'Please do it, Jack.'

Jack did. When he returned, he instinctively held the pillow between himself and the Ghost Mother.

She gazed at him solemnly. 'I used to hope – with all of my heart I used to hope – that I'd grow old before Isabella died. Can you imagine what the hope of a mother for a dying child might be like, Jack? How unyielding it would be? How resilient?'

Jack couldn't, but nodded to keep her calm.

'So, this is what I would do sometimes,' the Ghost Mother went on. 'I would daydream that when I looked in the mirror my hair had turned white. White, absolutely white. That I was grown old, yet my Isabella was still, somehow, alive. But death is stronger than love or dreams, Jack. Isabella was like a beautiful moon in wane, the slow way she faded from me, but she faded nonetheless. And toward the end, when I could no longer bear to see her suffering, I would often clutch a pillow to my chest much the way you are doing now. I would hold the fabric up to the light and consider what I might do with it, if I only had the courage. Do you understand what I am saying?'

'Jack!' Sarah called up again. 'How much longer do I have to wait? Everything's getting cold!'

'Answer her,' the Ghost Mother snapped. 'We don't want any interruptions.'

'One minute!' Jack managed to call down.

'Not one minute! Now! I mean it!'

The Ghost Mother glanced towards the staircase.

'Indulge me, Jack,' she said. 'This will not, after all, take more than a minute or so. Put the pillow against your face.'

'Against my face?'

65

'Yes. See what it feels like.'

Jack coughed twice, his throat closing slightly.

'Are you afraid, Jack?' the Ghost Mother said in an undertone. 'I'm a ghost, but I'm also a mother, or was once upon a time. What harm could I possibly do to you? Put it against your nose and lips.'

'No,' Jack said firmly.

'No?'

'No. I'm not going to do it. I won't.'

The Ghost Mother ran her hands across the pillow, as though she might force him to, then smiled and nodded. 'It is not a pleasant prospect, is it? I once put such a pillow against my own mouth, fastening it with ropes. I wanted to know what it would feel like if the time ever came when I decided out of mercy to use it on my beloved.'

'Jack?'

Sarah stood in the open doorway. She'd come up to tell Jack off, but as soon as she noticed the way he held the pillow she forgot about that. She saw the rocking chair, and the way he seemed to be listening.

'Jack, who are you talking to?'

'Me! Me! Me!' the Ghost Mother screamed. She glared at Sarah with naked hostility, her hands writhing in her lap. 'Is she truly a better parent than I was?' the Ghost Mother snarled. She turned angrily to Jack. 'If you had to, which mother would you choose? Me or her?'

'Her,' Jack said at once.

The Ghost Mother stared at Sarah with contempt, then retreated backwards out of the door, down the staircase and away.

'Jack, what's wrong?' Sarah asked.

Seizing his inhaler, Jack took a dosage and launched into everything that had happened. He tried to slow down, to make it believable, but the story included pillows, ropes and frightened, wispy children this time: it was wilder than ever. His attempts to reassure Sarah that it had nothing to do with his dad only made her more convinced it did. You idiot, he thought afterwards. You stupid, stupid idiot! Now look what you've done. You've really panicked her. She's so freaked out she's not even arguing with you.

Sarah waited until Jack was calmer. Then she said, 'We're leaving this place. Tomorrow morning. As soon as the doctor's examined you, and I'm sure it's safe for you to travel. I know you don't want to, Jack, but that's just what's got to happen. I'm sorry.'

For the next hour or so, Sarah never let Jack out of her sight. Three times she tested his peak flow number. On each occasion it was only borderline OK. There was a guarded silence between them over lunch and, seeing her expression, Jack knew he'd never change her mind about leaving. Even if he shut up about the dead people in the house for the rest of the day, her mind was obviously made up. She'd force him to go, and once the front door was locked would never allow him back.

In the afternoon, he asked if he could lie down, and she said yes, but insisted on staying with him until he fell asleep. Jack thought he wouldn't get any rest at all, but he did – wrestling with his asthma always exhausted him. And it was lucky that he did sleep, because when Jack woke again, hours later, Sarah had gone back to her own room, and someone else was near him.

It wasn't the Ghost Mother. The bedroom curtains were slightly parted, and through the dappled late afternoon sunshine, suspended in the air, there floated a boy.

Jack saw him clearly this time: a boy about his own age, with short blond wavy hair, wearing a red T-shirt. Jack could distinctly see freckles on the bridge of his nose, and for a moment he couldn't help thinking how comical freckles looked on a ghost. But when he looked more closely at the boy's face, Jack's smile faded.

'Oliver?' he whispered.

Overjoyed that Jack could see him, Oliver waved his arms. The waving motion lifted his body, buoying him up towards the window. The two boys stared at each other silently for a moment, only a few feet of sunshine and dust between them. Then Oliver started to shout at the top of his voice. Jack strained to hear, but couldn't. The words were too weakly spoken. No, it's not the boy's voice that's weak, Jack realized. It's his spirit. It's weaker than the Ghost Mother's. My gift isn't strong enough to pick it up yet.

Oliver stopped shouting, working on another method to communicate. He kept one eye on Jack, the other on the open doorway.

'The Ghost Mother?' Jack murmured. 'You don't want her seeing you? Is that why you're looking that way?'

Oliver nodded, and Jack closed the door. When he came back, Oliver had an idea and tried writing on the window with his finger.

'Wait,' Jack said, when Oliver's finger made no impression. 'Try this.'

Jack breathed on the window pane. His breath misted

up the glass. The condensation only lasted a few seconds before it evaporated, but that was enough for Oliver to hastily trace three words with his finger:

GRILL EBONY TREE

Jack shrugged. Was this supposed to be some sort of message? The words made no sense. 'In code?' he mouthed.

Oliver nodded. He wanted to write the words out plainly, but the risk that the Ghost Mother might slip in and see them was too great.

'OK, but what's the code?' Jack said. 'I don't understand.'

He breathed on the window again and Oliver wrote the same words. This time, though, he pointed at the first letter of each word:

GRILL EBONY TREE

Jack reached for a scrap of paper and a pen in his bedside drawer. Oliver waited impatiently, always keeping a close watch on the doorway, and when Jack was ready wrote one rapidly-dissolving word after another. This time he only stopped to let Jack renew his breath on the window pane:

GRILL EBONY TREE OWN USE TANK OTHER FREE
TONGUE HOUSE INTO SEA HILL OR US SHOOT EEL
OGRE REAL SLEEP HALL EACH LOSS LOUSE TALL
ROUND YOUNG TIP OUT HORROR UNDER REAL TIE
YELLOW OUTER UDDER

Jack looked over the message. Afterwards, he stared at Oliver and nodded bleakly. He didn't understand why Oliver had such a frightening message to convey, but he had no doubt the subject of the message was meant to be the Ghost Mother.

Oliver, elated at being understood, thumped his fists, though he still didn't take his eyes off the doorway. Jack wondered what risk he was taking to get this message to him. Or was the boy lying? The Ghost Mother had said the children would lie. No, he didn't think Oliver was lying.

'Tell me more,' Jack said. 'Your spirits aren't meant to be here, are they? Where should you all be?'

Oliver wrote:

TERROR HERO END ORDINARY THINK HEAR EAT RED
SMILE IDIOT DENT EAGLE

Jack stared at the words. Some distant part of him knew about this place, recognized it. He didn't want to wait for clumsy words on a window to find out more.

'I'm going to try something,' he told Oliver. 'Don't be scared. I've never done it before, but the Ghost Mother showed me. Stay where you are.'

Jack put his hand out to Oliver's face.

Oliver was surprised, almost pulled away, but Jack coaxed him forward. He had no idea how to extract what he needed from Oliver's mind, but he knew he had to find a memory that would tell him more about this house. It wasn't easy. He wasn't sure how much of Oliver he needed to touch. More than just his hand, he discovered. He had to press his whole body against Oliver. Uncomfortable,

Oliver started to drift away – then their minds connected.

It was a fairly recent memory. Somehow, even before it began, Jack knew it was going to be about the death of the old woman who had last been in the farmhouse.

He saw this: her arthritic hands, holding a book. It was a cool, late June evening and she was in bed, the four ghost children, including Oliver, gathered beside her, reading with her as she turned the pages of a novel. She'd reached page 257 when she abruptly – stopped. She removed her reading glasses, and stared in an unfocused way out of the window. 'Oh,' she murmured, almost laughing at a tiny pain shooting through her chest, it was so small.

She put the book down. She did not mark the place as usual. She reached for the frame of the bed, but her trembling hand never made it there. Just for a moment her face twitched painfully, and then she lay still.

The four ghost children huddled together to watch what occurred next. But it was no real surprise to them. It was no surprise at all. They knew exactly what would happen. They knew because it had happened to each of them when they died.

The old woman's *loved ones* came for her.

There were many of them after such a long life: her deceased friends, departed family members, even a long-dead childhood companion who'd waited a whole lifetime to greet her again. All those who had known and cared about her before they died, came now. Just as the loved ones of Ann, Charlie, Gwyneth and Oliver had reached for them at the instant of their death, so those of the old woman came to ease her away to the Other Side.

And her spirit went with them. Willingly, easily, she

raised her hands to the loved ones, and as she did so they swept her from her wizened body and carried her away. But, just before she passed beyond to the Other Side, she briefly saw the ghost children. All those years she had lived with them as intimate acquaintances, never suspecting they were with her. But now, a spirit herself, she saw them standing in their death-clothes on her bed. And they were screaming.

'Please! Let me go with you! I'm Gwyneth! Don't you see me?'

'Take me as well! Don't leave me here!' cried Charlie, lifting his emaciated arms and shouting out his mother's name.

But it was Oliver's reaction that was the most extreme. His own loved ones had come for him only eleven years before, and the memory was still like a fresh wound. Not caring what the other children thought of him, he rode the air currents up to the plaster on the ceiling, pressed his face there, and pleaded, promising anything, anything if only the old woman's loved ones would take him with them as well.

But the old woman was lifted up and away. Her loved ones could do nothing for the children: they had eyes only for the one they loved; they could not even see the other spirits in the house. And so the children were left behind again.

Oliver, in Jack's room, backed away, shaking.

'There is only one chance for the loved ones to take you, isn't there?' Jack said, beginning to understand. 'At the instant of death. Only then. That is when it is meant to take place. If anything stops your loved ones reaching you at that moment, they can't come back.'

Oliver nodded grimly.

'Did the Ghost Mother stop them carrying you away?'

Another nod.

'How? She's done something to you, hasn't she? She brought you to this house, and now she's stopped you leaving. Is that right?'

SNAKE HATE

Oliver stopped at the beginning of the sentence, and Jack sensed why: the Ghost Mother was nearby. They could both detect her, slinking up the staircase. Clearly anxious to leave, Oliver beckoned Jack to breathe on the window one last time, and delayed long enough to write the following words:

SNAKE HATE EACH SILENT THIEF ON LOSE ENDED OWN UNDER RETURN SKIN OTHER UNDONE LEAF SHINE

Nine

Isabella

After Oliver left, Jack had an overwhelming desire to make sure his mum was safe. He checked her room and found her still asleep, breathing shallowly. To keep her safe meant leaving – Oliver's first message had been clear enough. But what the Ghost Mother had done to the children sounded even more frightening. Jack couldn't just leave in the morning without knowing what it meant. Of course, if it was true, the Ghost Mother would only deny it. She might even punish Oliver for telling him. The answers, he sensed, were somehow linked to Isabella's death.

Jack didn't delay this time. He carried Isabella's rocking chair back into his own bedroom, and sat in it. Let the Ghost Mother erupt in anger if she wanted; he was better prepared now if she did.

But as soon as he touched the hard wooden seat, all thoughts of the Ghost Mother were banished from Jack's mind. Instead, another place murmured its existence – a distant place Jack had been on the verge of discovering since his dad passed away.

'The Other Side,' he whispered, remembering Oliver's words.

It was real: he could feel it; in balance with the living world, a world of the dead; a dimension beyond; and it was a warm place, not cold or distant; an existence where the dead were welcomed. Jack gripped the chair, and as he did so all the billions of souls on the Other Side began to open up to him. And, amongst them, one particular soul, special to Jack.

'Dad,' he gasped. 'Dad!'

He could not hear or see his father, but he sensed him there, on the Other Side, waiting for him.

Jack trembled, all thoughts of the Ghost Mother gone. Could he somehow make contact with his dad? Was it possible to find a way to reach out to the Other Side, even find a way to bring him back?

Even as the idea blossomed in his mind, some part of Jack recognized that he was not meant to – that souls should not be drawn from the Other Side, not even his dad.

But Jack couldn't help himself. If there was a possibility, he had to try. Nothing else mattered in that moment. I'll only take one soul from there, he thought. And not for long. Just to say goodbye. Closing his eyes, easing back in the rocking chair, Jack willed his father back from the dead.

But it was not his father who came.

*

Jack did not notice the moment Isabella's spirit appeared in our world. She arrived unseen, like a tranquil sound from a far place, and shivered behind Jack, getting used to the eeriness of being amongst the living again. Frightened, but recognizing that this was a room from her old house, she ran her hands down her torso. Her body was even more tenuous than those of the ghost children. It had no strength, and just the surface appearance of flesh. Even so, no spiritualist armed with séances or other crafts had ever possessed a talent to summon the dead in quite the same way as Jack, and though Isabella should never have made it so fully back, she had. His gift had shattered all the rules. The boundaries between the worlds were only ever meant to be broken when a person died, and their loved ones arrived from the Other Side to take them away. But Jack alone had summoned Isabella. His gift was unique, and there were no precedents for what would happen next.

Isabella stared wildly at him, afraid of Jack and of being here: what did it mean? A boy had summoned her! A boy no older than she had done this! Isabella knew little about boys. Throughout those few years she had been well enough to attend school during her short life, boys were rigidly segregated from girls. After that, she had only glimpsed them occasionally from her room.

She glanced nervously at Jack, then took a moment to gaze out of the window. For years, from her rocking chair, she had stared out from this very window into the garden. In those days her mother had cultivated forget-me-nots, cowslip, foxgloves and coltsfoot for her, scented blue violet and rambling rose. All were gone now, replaced by weeds. Yet the sun was in the sky, and trees swayed in a mild summer breeze. Seeing the distant ripening corn fields, Isabella held back a gasp.

So beautiful, she thought. Oh, I'd forgotten . . .

How extraordinary it felt to be alive again, even this peculiar half-life! The Other Side had its own wonders and glories, but nothing like the sight of wind through corn. Isabella shuddered, spotting a mirror on one wall of the room. She wasn't sure she wanted to look into it, but she did. It was her death-look she saw there, the final bitter expression. She spent some time pulling her face around, trying to improve it. Then she saw Jack staring at her.

'Isabella!' he murmured.

'Not what you expected, eh?' she replied, more boldly than she felt. 'Meddling with death, without knowing what you are doing? Got more than you bargained for, boy?'

Her voice, to Jack, was like sand through fingers. Her dark brown eyes, looking into his, could not have been wider. A cream linen nightgown reached down to her bare feet, and he could tell from her narrow ankles how thin her legs must be. Her hair was shockingly rich next to her pale skin. And how much of her was really in the room? He could see her, but Isabella was still more air than substance. When she turned her body, Jack could barely follow her outline.

'I wanted . . . my dad,' he told her, introducing himself. 'I didn't mean to bring –'

'Me?' she interrupted. 'But you were holding the *chair*. It was me it powerfully linked you to. And now that I am here, speak quickly if you have anything to say, for the Other Side will not let me remain long.' She coughed once, a horrible gravelly sound that made Jack wince. In response to his look, she wiped her mouth and smiled knowingly. 'It is nothing,' she said. 'Just my graveyard cough. I am used to it. We lived many years together, it and I.'

For a moment they appraised each other, neither sure what to say or do next.

'You . . . you died of consumption, didn't you?' Jack whispered at last. 'It must have been terrible.'

'Terrible?' Isabella shot Jack a sharp look, still wary of him. 'Is that why you called my soul back, then? To discuss death? You enjoy the stuff of death, do you? I'll tell you, then, what it was like. It was like having a mouse in my chest – a mouse that would not stop gnawing. Well? Does that satisfy you?'

'No, you don't understand. I . . .' Jack hesitated. Then, thinking of his dad, he asked the only question that seemed to matter in that moment.

'Tell me what it's like to exist on the Other Side, Isabella?'

'I cannot tell you about that,' she replied.

'Why not?'

'In good time, you will discover what it is like for yourself.' She smiled, softening a little. 'Not too soon, I hope.' Tapping her lips thoughtfully, she said, 'Jack, if it is only for such idle questions you have brought me back here, let me go. I must return to the Other Side. I do not belong here; none of the dead do. Please . . .'

But she broke off, her plea to leave only half-hearted. Jack could see that the last thing she wanted to do was to leave. She kept gazing longingly around the room, a look of wonder, as if she missed everything. Seeing that, Jack relaxed slightly. He had far too many unanswered questions to want her to leave yet. In any case, he found her fascinating. She stared intently out of the window, as if stunned by the beauty of the world.

'The colours, Jack,' she sighed. 'The tastes. The smells, even the ugly ones. The Other Side has its own virtues, but nothing like these things.' She stretched out her arms, sighed again. 'And air! Wonderful air! Breathe it while you may, even if I cannot!' She tried to draw in a great lungful, failed, coughed heavily, suddenly laughed, tried for another lungful, laughed again. 'I read about my illness, you know,' she said. 'Mother taught me to read beyond primers. I read the medical text. It said, "The cheeks, in the end, are hollow, the eyes commonly sunken in their sockets, and often look morbidly bright and staring."' She gazed at him, and laughed again. 'Do my eyes not look morbidly bright and staring?'

Jack had to admit they did.

'Well, that's all over now,' she said, 'and I will not fear death a second time, for what little time I am permitted to stay here in the realm of the living. Do you fear for your own death, Jack?' she asked quietly, moving towards him. 'Is that what has made you summon me?' She attempted to cradle Jack's face in both her hands, but her wrists, thin as an infant's, passed through him. She laughed down at them. 'Death is only the beginning of something better,' she muttered in his ear. 'Don't fear it, like so many of us did.'

Breaking contact again, she strode across the room.

Jack was enthralled by her. He'd expected a feeble, shy girl when she first appeared, not this vibrant force. From the light of the window he could see the bony shoulders through her dress. She is beautiful, he thought. Or at one time she was. Her mother was right about that.

'Isabella,' he said. 'My dad . . . can you tell me anything about . . .'

'He misses you.' Isabella murmured it so quietly that Jack barely heard.

A tingle ran up his spine.

'How do you know that?'

'Do you think the loved ones on the Other Side are not aware of one another? Of course we are. What is your last memory of him?'

'I . . . I never saw Dad the night he died,' Jack said. 'I . . . was out, with people from school. I wasn't even enjoying myself.' He faltered. Isabella edged closer, urging him to continue. 'But something, I don't know what, made me come home. And then Mum was there, waiting at the door . . .'

Isabella said gently, 'Was your father still in the house when you returned?'

'No. They'd taken him. I heard later that he'd been in the house a long time, waiting for the ambulance. He died in the ambulance . . . but it took a long time for that as well. I . . . can tell from what Mum told me that he was conscious for most of the journey, holding on. I could have been with him, but I wasn't . . .'

Isabella knelt beside Jack, nodding almost imperceptibly.

'Perhaps you were fortunate in being away when he departed,' she said. 'It is possible to see too much. On the day before my father's death, I saw the blood gush forth from his mouth. Even then, however, he had the presence of mind not only to commend himself to God, but to take up with his own hands a basin that lay at our bedside and put it beneath his lips. When the morning came and he found that he was still alive, Mother and I both wept. Oh, Jack, you have no idea what it was like. He'd been a strong man, but in the end he lay in Mother's arms as light as a babe, breathing with the utmost difficulty, so tired he could not even speak. He raised his voice once more only, in his final hours, to say my name and Mother's. He did not realize we were already there, by his bedside. And then, at eight o'clock that morning, he passed away, so quietly we both thought he had fallen asleep.'

Jack lowered his gaze.

'I remember what Mother did next,' Isabella said. 'She slept. She had not slept for days, but she laid her head down next to me, took Father's still-warm hand, and mine, and fell asleep.'

Light from the window shone on Isabella.

'You know, don't you?' Jack said. He'd been so shocked to find her in the room that he'd not even thought to ask. 'Isabella, you do know that your mother is still here in this house?'

'Still here?' Isabella stared at him in disbelief, almost laughed. 'That cannot be, Jack. When Mother died, Father and I went together to take her spirit to the Other Side. She refused to come with us – I am still unsure why – but there is only one place she could go after that.'

'What do you mean?'

'If a spirit does not follow the loved ones across to the Other Side at the moment of death, it is stuck in the living world, Jack. There it gradually fades. It fades until there is no energy left of its soul, and then it is claimed by a place of which I do not wish to speak. The *Nightmare Passage*, we call it. It is a dreadful place, cold, terrifying. Only tortured, guilt-ridden souls who refuse to go to the Other Side when their loved ones come for them end up there, or any poor souls they take with them. By now Mother must be inside the Nightmare Passage. She could not have survived this length of time and still be in your world.'

'What if she's using other souls in this house to keep her from fading?'

'Others?'

'Children. Your mother *is* here, Isabella, and the souls of four dead children are with her. She's done something to them, trapped their souls in the house.'

'Their what?' Isabella stood up, her face suddenly filled with horror.

Jack stood up with her. 'What has she done to them, Isabella? Why are you so scared?'

'No,' Isabella said, clutching at the collar of her gown. 'No. It cannot be. You must be . . . mistaken. I cannot believe she would do that, trap them that way. There is no worse crime for a spirit left on this earth than to use another to keep itself out of the Nightmare Passage. Oh, Mother, surely you haven't . . . surely . . .'

'Talk to her!' Jack said. 'She's your mother, isn't she? She'll listen to you.'

Isabella shook her head. 'Those on the Other Side cannot communicate with the dead stuck in this world, Jack. Oh, Mother, you haven't, have you?' Tears lined her eyes. 'Was it too many years alone, with only spiders and mice as friends? What happened to you, Mother? What did you become?' She held her hands to her lips. 'Jack, listen to me. You must —' She gasped.

Jack knew the reason at once. A counter-force was beckoning – the Other Side, drawing her back again.

'No!' Isabella cried, unable to resist it.

'Not yet!' Jack begged. 'Please. I need —'

'Oh, Jack, I can't stay. I . . .' Isabella's forlorn whisper was already distant. Her body flickered like a transparency against the window as she tried to hold herself in the room. 'If I can, I will return to help you,' she cried. 'Jack! I —'

'Don't leave! You can't leave! I need to know what to do!'

But Isabella was already gone. For minutes afterwards Jack stayed in the same spot, still feeling the echoes of her presence in the room. Then, before they were completely gone, he ran across to the window, to look out at the beauty of the world with the same fierceness Isabella had done.

Ten

Bargaining for Souls

'Why won't the Ghost Mother leave Oliver alone?'

'She'll give up chasing him soon, like she always does,' Ann answered Charlie.

'You said that before, and she's still chasing him!'

'But she hasn't caught him, has she?'

Ann had carefully concealed herself, Charlie and Gwyneth in the dark seclusion of the scullery. It had the advantage of plenty of shadows to blend into, but if they were discovered the only escape route was via the kitchen. From the speed of the Ghost Mother's movements about the house, Ann could tell how furious she must be with Oliver. Obviously she'd seen him warn Jack. None of them would be forgiven for that, least of all Ann.

Gwyneth counted feverishly. It was what she always did to take her mind off the Ghost Mother. Every time she felt one of the tell-tale tremors marking the Ghost Mother's passage between the rooms, she clutched Ann and started again.

'Two, three, four . . .'

Charlie was frantic. 'The Ghost Mother's going to get Oliver this time! She's *never* chased him for this long before.'

'No, he'll get away,' Ann reassured him. 'He's faster than her. He's staying ahead.'

'We won't be safe!' Gwyneth whimpered. 'If she can't catch Oliver, she'll come after us. Oliver wasn't meant to let her see him. He's made her mad. She always finds us when she's really mad! It's Oliver's fault.'

'Shut up!' Charlie growled. 'It's *you* who'll give us away, not him!'

'Quiet,' Ann said. 'It's not Oliver's fault. Anyway, she's too interested in the new boy to pay much attention to us.'

But Ann did not really believe her own words. Dormant for so many years, the Ghost Mother was active again. Moving about the house taxed her energy. Chasing Oliver would tax it further. Ann knew it was only a matter of time before she came after their souls for more of it. And then the usual screaming and bargaining would start.

Avoiding detection depended on keeping Gwyneth calm. She panicked when the Ghost Mother was close. No matter how well Ann prepared her, she always did.

'Two, three, four, I will not see her, she will not come, I will not see her . . .'

Seeing the dread already rising in Gwyneth's eyes, Charlie glanced nervously towards the scullery entrance.

'Help her,' Ann said, to keep him occupied. 'Get her to use larger numbers and count more slowly. It makes her concentrate better.'

The Ghost Mother was close. From somewhere in the

kitchen, they caught a scrap of her threat to Oliver. 'For meddling, I won't just take part of your soul. I'll take whatever's left, the whole of it.' Oliver laughed, but the laugh wasn't convincing.

'She won't do that, will she?' Charlie asked.

Ann shook her head. 'No, of course not.'

'I'd rather she took me instead.'

Ann glanced down, knowing Charlie meant it. Oliver was everything to him.

'She's coming,' Gwyneth whimpered. 'Four, five . . .'

Ann held her. 'Even if she's close she won't know we're in here if we keep still, remember? Stay really, really quiet. Please, Gwyneth . . . shush, now . . .'

Oliver, staying just ahead of the Ghost Mother, tried to taunt her away from their location. 'Hey! Can't chase me down? Giving up? You're useless! Here, I'll give you a chance! How close do you need me to be?'

But it was too late. The Ghost Mother had drifted near enough to the scullery to sense the other children's presence. Once that happened she ignored Oliver's jeers and floated towards them on a thread of stale air. She hovered inside the doorway. There she waited, her eyes adjusting to the meagre light, listening.

For a moment it looked as if the ghost children might be safe. The Ghost Mother was confused, because Gwyneth, unusually, kept quiet. She counted only in her mind, as Ann had taught her to do when she was really frightened. But the Ghost Mother knew Gwyneth's weakness only too well, and simply waited her out.

Seconds ticked by, Oliver mocked and heckled from tantalizingly close range, and still Gwyneth held her nerve

– the longest she had ever lasted. But the Ghost Mother bided her time, and finally Gwyneth cracked, her mouth slowly opening in a silent scream. Seeing that, Ann did what she always did when it was too late. First, she reached over and placed Gwyneth's hand in Charlie's, putting him in charge of her. Then she floated out in plain sight of the Ghost Mother, offering herself.

Oliver felt a sickening lurch. Two or three times before he'd watched Ann submitting herself this same way. He couldn't bear to watch it again. He didn't know that in private Ann had done so many more times, but spared him the sight.

'Don't let her!' he begged. 'Ann, no, please . . .'

'It's all right,' she replied. 'Stay back. I know what I'm doing. Don't interfere.'

The last thing Ann wanted was for Oliver to risk everything in an attempt to help her. He didn't understand the special arrangement played out between her and the Ghost Mother. None of them realized that she had been secretly visiting the Ghost Mother for decades, doing what she needed to do to keep her away from Charlie and Gwyneth. On most of those visits, Ann was only required to be a silent companion – a child on a rocking chair, sitting in a cellar. Other times she let her hair be plaited, or sat in the dark while the Ghost Mother talked soothingly and fussed over her as if she was as ill as Isabella had been. Isabella. The dear one. The beloved. Oh yes. Over the years Ann had learned all about her. Occasionally, when the Ghost Mother was in one of her most dangerous, predatory moods, Ann even tried to sound like her. It was the only way of keeping the Ghost Mother away from Gwyneth on such days. She'd learned that a breathless voice worked best.

Sometimes, though, even that wasn't enough. When the Ghost Mother's energy was low, the Nightmare Passage threatening to take her, she came directly instead to steal a part of Ann's soul. And Ann gave it. Even though it terrified her, she had no choice; if she didn't the Ghost Mother would only take what she needed from the youngsters. She couldn't allow that.

Oliver, of course, was able to take care of himself.

'Don't get involved,' Ann warned him now. 'Don't come any nearer, Oliver!' But she knew he would. His blood was up from the chase. She had to control him or he'd madden the Ghost Mother. If he did that the Ghost Mother might break her long-standing agreement with Ann, always to go to her first when she needed renewing.

'Take the others away!' she ordered Oliver. 'I don't want them here. Gwyneth, Charlie, leave now.'

They did so, holding hands, edging around the floor as far from the Ghost Mother as possible.

The Ghost Mother pretended not to notice them. She was focused on Ann.

'You know what I need,' she said.

'Of course. Be quiet. Wait until they're gone.'

'Ann, don't!' Oliver shouted.

'Go away!' Ann snarled. 'Leave us alone! Just this once, Oliver, do as I ask!'

Swearing at the Ghost Mother, Oliver roughly picked up Charlie and Gwyneth and helped navigate them out into the kitchen. The Ghost Mother flowed towards Ann before they were out of sight.

'Not yet,' Ann said. 'Remember our agreement. Not in front of the others.'

The Ghost Mother nodded with ill-concealed impatience.

Ann waited until Gwyneth was far enough away to get to safety before she let the Ghost Mother come any closer.

'Are you ready?' the Ghost Mother asked.

'Yes,' Ann replied.

'I will give you a moment to prepare yourself.'

They were alone together, in the quiet privacy of the scullery. The last time the Ghost Mother had removed any of Ann's soul had been over a year earlier. On that occasion she'd only siphoned off the usual quantity, just enough to keep her spirit in the house. Over the decades, Ann had successfully rationed the Ghost Mother this way, convincing her that taking small amounts was the best way to keep her own soul for as long as possible out of the Nightmare Passage.

In return for Ann's co-operation, the Ghost Mother left Charlie and Gwyneth alone – usually. Sometimes she took some of their soul anyway, and whenever the Ghost Mother did that she removed a lot, because Charlie and Gwyneth screamed and excited her, and she lost herself in the action.

If she fully co-operated, left them alone, Ann allowed the Ghost Mother a special treat – an extra visit, perhaps, or, sometimes, letting the Ghost Mother hide close to Charlie and Gwyneth and watch them playing. The Ghost Mother liked that, especially being near Gwyneth, make-believing she was a reborn little Isabella. Charlie and Gwyneth rarely knew they were being watched, but

Oliver did. He'd never been convinced to bargain with the Ghost Mother. His ability to use the house breezes was so masterly that she'd never caught him yet. But, if she ever did, Ann knew that for all his taunting over the years the Ghost Mother wouldn't hold back. She'd drain the whole of his soul, take it all. She wouldn't be able to resist.

Today, Ann saw, was going to hurt. The Ghost Mother looked in no mood to restrict her appetite. The new boy, Jack, clearly excited her beyond belief.

As the Ghost Mother dipped her face closer, Ann stared straight ahead. 'Don't take too much,' she said, hating how feeble she sounded. 'I am . . . already close to the Nightmare Passage.'

The Ghost Mother drew back. 'You have felt it?'

'Yes.'

'What was it like?'

'Like a cold lip on my heart.'

The Ghost Mother nodded, satisfied that Ann wasn't lying.

Ann had never forgotten her only glimpse of the Nightmare Passage. She'd seen a child's soul enter it, a boy – eleven-year-old Daniel. When the Ghost Mother first captured Ann, and took her back to the farmhouse, Daniel's soul was already there. He'd been trapped for many years already. Gradually Ann saw his energy dwindle, until the Nightmare Passage came to claim him. Ann always blamed herself for that. She could have delayed the moment. But Daniel had a rebellious spirit, like Oliver, and she'd enjoyed that, and actively encouraged him to resist. As a result, Daniel's spirit faded faster.

'I am coming towards you now,' the Ghost Mother said.

Ann nodded. She had learned that it was best not to resist the Ghost Mother at these times. If she did, the Ghost Mother only went berserk and took more. Better to pretend a little affection – or at least acceptance. Not to cringe when she came too close.

Oliver hated to see Ann submit this way, but he didn't understand. He thought nothing could be worse than allowing the Ghost Mother to slowly feed off their souls. Ann knew better. The Nightmare Passage was worse. Even this miserable life – playing hide-and-seek around the house, avoiding the Ghost Mother as often as they could – was better than anything awaiting them in the Nightmare Passage. Eventually their souls would all end up there, of course, but Ann did what she could to delay that moment. Ever since Gwyneth's and Charlie's spirits had been dragged into the house, her efforts had gone into shielding them from the Ghost Mother's appetite as best she could.

But the price was high. The price was her own soul.

'Do the others realize you are close to the Nightmare Passage?' the Ghost Mother asked.

'Only Oliver.'

'Why haven't you told Charlie and Gwyneth?'

'Why should I?'

That's what you'd have done, isn't it? Ann thought. Frightened them. Used them to gain a little sympathy, then sacrificed them to save yourself, as you always do. But Ann didn't say this. The Ghost Mother was impulsive enough. Better to give her everything she needed without objecting. However, part of Ann wanted to delay the moment the Ghost Mother started to feed. She couldn't help that.

'Do you remember Daniel?' she asked, stirring up the oldest memory between them.

The Ghost Mother took her time to recall. 'Yes,' she said eventually. 'How could I forget? Of all of you, Daniel was most like Oliver. When I left the house, and found him in that town, he fought me hard. I was lucky to be able to fend off his loved ones when the moment came. I had to dig my nails into his soul for a long time before they left, and I could bring him back here.'

'He entered the Nightmare Passage forty-two years ago.'

'That long?' The Ghost Mother pondered a moment. 'Well, he was my first soul. I did not know how to ration myself. If I had not made such a mistake, he might still be here for me to feed from. You taught me a great deal, Ann. I am grateful for that, and for what you are about to give me now.' She faced her expectantly. 'Well?'

'I'm ready.'

Ann straightened out her slip. The Ghost Mother approached, enveloping her in her arms. It was the clumsy, almost sentimental, way she preferred, and Ann allowed it. Then, knowing what was next, she parted her lips. The Ghost Mother took hold of Ann's head, twisting it this way and that, until she found the best angle, a good seal on her mouth. Ann did not resist her. It was easier this way. She didn't want the Ghost Mother to have to fight her; it would only make her take more.

Ann's energy shot into the Ghost Mother, and the Ghost Mother convulsed. Closing her eyes in disgust, Ann felt the ripples through her body, the emptying, but did not pull away. It was difficult, but over the years she had learned not to scream. The pain was more bearable once the flow was underway, but at the start it was always hard.

This time, however, felt worse than usual; something was wrong.

'Wait,' she tried to say, but the seal on her lips was too tight.

She struggled to pull away. The Ghost Mother grunted, holding her more tightly.

What was happening? The flow felt different. And then Ann realized what was wrong. Already weakened after all the years of giving, she had almost nothing left. For the first time, Ann's soul was truly close to entering the Nightmare Passage.

'No!' she begged, trying to pull her lips away.

The Ghost Mother pressed herself closer, not ready to end the feeding yet.

'*What . . . what are you doing?*'

A voice from the kitchen.

It was Jack, in disbelief, unable to comprehend what he was seeing. He'd heard whispering, and arrived to see the Ghost Mother's face attached to the mouth of a teenage girl with long red hair. He saw Ann pull her face away from the distracted Ghost Mother, and something leak out of her mouth. Then Ann quickly jumped on a breeze that took her beyond Jack into the kitchen. 'Thank you,' she murmured brokenly, as she floated past him.

The Ghost Mother wiped her lips, an obscene gesture, obviously wanting to follow Ann, but held rooted by whatever Jack made of this.

Fluttering, nervous, she eyed him warily.

'I saw you doing something to her face,' he said. 'What was it?'

'Nothing, Jack. She was . . . unharmed, as you saw.'

'Unharmed?' Jack watched Ann drifting with difficulty down the corridor, a hand across her mouth. Oliver came back, lifting Ann in his arms, his face anguished. Then he soared away along the corridor, holding Ann's head up.

Jack turned back to the Ghost Mother.

'Whatever the children told you earlier is untrue,' she said. 'I warned you about them, Jack.'

'They say you have their souls.'

'That is not so.'

'I know about the Nightmare Passage.' He watched her face twitch with fear. 'You left this house, found their souls and used them somehow to keep you out of it, didn't you?'

The Ghost Mother said nothing.

Jack stepped towards her, determined to grasp her wrists, find out that way if she wouldn't tell him voluntarily.

She swayed away. 'It's . . . a lie, Jack. I haven't hurt them.'

'Haven't you?'

She stared at him, a pitiful look asking for forgiveness.

'I'll never love you,' Jack said. 'And I'll never call you mother. You know that, don't you? I'll never do it. Let their souls go!'

The Ghost Mother shook her head. 'Don't blame me. Please . . .' Her face crumpled. 'Please, Jack, don't hate me. I can see it in your eyes. Please . . .'

'If you let them go, I'll try to help you. I'll stay with you if I can.'

'Stay with me? Oh, but Sarah will not change her mind about leaving tomorrow, Jack. That is not going to happen, is it?' Her face was suddenly resigned. 'In any case, what hope do I have that you will truly love me now you have seen this?' She sighed deeply, turning her back on him. 'Soon you will be gone,' she muttered. 'And once you are, nothing will have changed. It will be just me and the ghost children again, living together as we always have these past years. You have broken my heart, Jack, but I have become acquainted with many such disappointments and lacerations of the heart. Yes, I can live with this one as well.'

She drifted away, slipping beyond his reach.

'No. Don't leave yet,' Jack said. 'Let me help you. I want to. I want to understand!'

He followed her as she floated out into the corridor towards the staircase.

Oliver, with Ann lying in his arms, slipped down the banister to the lower part of the house. The Ghost Mother flowed up the staircase, for once not chasing him. Jack couldn't follow both the children and the Ghost Mother. After an agonizing moment of indecision, he chose to follow the Ghost Mother.

'Don't leave now,' he begged, as she headed away. 'Please. I have to talk to you. I need to!' His voice was frayed – the asthma acting up again. Stopped from following her by a sharp pain in his chest, he reached out an arm to the Ghost Mother. She did not look back at him. Rising, she slipped under a crack between the stairs and entered a part of the house where Jack could never follow. He stood there, thumping the stairs in frustration, asthma building in his lungs.

When he next looked up, Sarah was staring down at him from the landing.

Eleven

Between the Lips

How does a mother protect her child from something she cannot understand? Sarah saw only this: Jack crazily bashing the stairs, pleading at the empty air, screaming over and over for a ghost to come back to talk to him. As he rushed through his story, it was the sheer detail of the world Jack had constructed for himself that dismayed her more than anything. What a terrible mistake, coming to this old house, she thought. It had only worsened the grief he felt over his father's death. The expression of heartfelt certainty on Jack's face when he told her his dad's spirit was still alive somewhere nearly made her cry.

Obviously, they had to get out of this house. She would have left at once, there and then, except Jack was bound to resist, and she didn't dare risk a physical struggle with him right now. His breathing was erratic, out of control, on the verge of another asthma attack. If he had a second major attack so soon after the last the consequences could be appalling. Somehow she had to keep him calm. So she lied. She told him what he wanted to hear. She pretended that if he got some genuine rest, real sleep, she'd consider staying.

'Really?' Jack could tell she didn't mean it. 'Mum, I'm not making this up. I'm not! It's all true.'

'I'll think about staying, all right? I'm not promising anything. But there can't be any more sneaking around the house. I want you in your room, resting.'

'All right, I will, I will.'

'And you'll sleep?'

'Yeah, I'll . . . I'll try.'

'And no more wandering around the house?'

'OK.'

'I mean it, Jack. You've just got to let your chest get some rest.'

Jack stared at her, his shoulders slumping. There was no point going along with the pretence that they were going to stay. Where would that get him?

'Mum, we're leaving tomorrow, aren't we? You've already decided. You aren't going to change your mind, are you?'

'Jack . . . I know you're convinced that —'

'Yes, but you don't believe me! You don't, do you?'

'I just think . . .' She hesitated, trying to find a phrase that would keep him calm. '. . . that we ought to get away from here, only a few days, that's all —'

'No! It won't just be for a few days, will it? You'll never let me come back once we're out of here. I know you won't!'

'Jack —'

'Mum, you're wrong! I'm not obsessing over Dad. I'm not. If you'd seen how scared that girl ghost looked you'd do everything you could to help her. It's not OK to leave the ghost children here. We've got to do something to help them. The Mother had her face up against her, and she was –'

'OK, calm down, calm down.' Please, please, she thought. This argument was stupid, only inflaming his asthma. 'Look, the doctor's coming late tomorrow morning,' she said, in a tone to end the discussion. 'Let's see what he's got to say. We'll talk more about it then.'

Jack stared at her sullenly, trying to come up with an argument to change her mind. I'll beg and plead, he thought. Whatever I need to do to stay. But even as he thought that, Jack knew his mum had the upper hand. After the asthma attacks, she was physically stronger than him. If she wanted to manhandle him out of the house he'd have trouble stopping her.

He allowed himself to be led upstairs, anxious to co-operate about the sleeping if there was any chance it might make any difference to her decision. In any case, he was genuinely exhausted. She was right: too much asthma, not enough catch-up rest. All he wanted to do was go on another search for the ghosts, but he'd only be staggering about or worse if he didn't get some rest first.

He slipped into his pyjamas and lay on his side, the best position for his lungs. Sarah placed her hands on his shoulder blades, to focus him. It was a method she'd used endless times in the aftermath of asthma attacks, and Jack made himself relax into it. There was no point trying to fake sleep. She'd know. To the sounds of birds singing outside the window, he let the solid warm pressure of her fingers send him off.

While Sarah stayed with Jack, the Ghost Mother waited outside, unable to bear the thought of seeing any tenderness between the two of them. It was only after Sarah left that she sneaked through the open door. Jack was sleeping and, seeing that, the Ghost Mother smiled. He'd said some hurtful things about not loving her earlier, but there was no point letting that spoil their final precious hours together.

How long would she have alone with Jack before Sarah came back? No way to tell. The Ghost Mother hoped she would have at least the early evening with him all to herself. It was as good a time to be with him as any, a gentle warmth slanting across his cheekbones, showing his features off at their finest. Soon the sun would set, and the shadows grow, but even then she would stay near him. Like his own true mother, she would watch over him. And that was appropriate for, after all, hadn't she once been a mother herself? Now she was a Ghost Mother, but her desire to care for a child was no less strong than that of the live one striding around so anxiously downstairs.

Jack dozed on into the evening, and Sarah, grateful, didn't wake him. Instead, she made arrangements with a friend to stay the following night, then packed a couple of bags so that they could leave as soon as the doctor gave Jack the all-clear tomorrow. She couldn't wait to leave now. It wasn't possible to enjoy a moment in the house after hearing Jack's bizarre story. Stuffing a raincoat into a rucksack, she even caught herself looking up sharply at her reflection in the hall mirror, as if one of his ghosts might be there.

'Stop it,' she told herself. 'Don't be ridiculous.'

Later, she crept up to Jack's room and listened. Even from outside the door she could tell he was lying down, on his side. With relief she noticed that his breathing was more regular, the wheeze gone altogether. She listened for a hesitation, any kind of catch in his throat that might represent an underlying problem. Nothing. He was sleeping soundly.

Tiptoeing back downstairs, she finished packing. Tonight I'll bring my mattress and sleep in Jack's room whether he likes it or not, she thought. Making herself a cappuccino and a bite to eat, she wandered into the lounge. The fire still glowed faintly and she threw on a last log. For a while she perched edgily on the sofa, looking round for something to occupy her. Then she went to check on Jack again. She was relieved to find him still sleeping. Snoring, in fact. Hearing that, she relaxed for the first time that day. She went back downstairs and lay on the sofa, stretching out her tense back muscles. The fire was almost gutted, and the lounge fairly dark.

The Ghost Mother sighed, listening to Jack gently snoring. A boy's snore. Nothing ugly about it. You could hardly hear it at all. My last hours with him, she thought. My very, very last. But as the minutes ticked by, and the sun dipped like a last chance below the horizon, the Ghost Mother became increasingly anxious. She tried to resign herself to it, but in truth she couldn't bear to think of Jack no longer being with her in the house. He was a real boy, not an ethereal spirit like the ghost children. Anyway, the others all despised her. Even Ann, the only one who made any effort to comfort her, had little soul-energy left. She'd soon end up in the Nightmare Passage, followed in time by Charlie and Gwyneth. The prospect of being left alone in the house with only Oliver to try to seek affection from was unbearable.

Leaving Jack's room, the Ghost Mother floated down-stairs. Sarah sat in front of the fire, nursing her coffee. The Ghost Mother brooded nearby, hating her.

'It isn't fair that you should have him all to yourself!' she howled. 'How dare you take him from me!'

Sarah wandered into the kitchen. Restless, needing something to do, she slid on rubber gloves, smeared bleach on a scouring pad and wiped the nearest surface clean.

The Ghost Mother had seen others before her in the house using such modern cleansing agents. 'Do you know what I had?' she muttered enviously. 'Soap, turps and pipe clay mashed into a paste!' But she couldn't hold onto her bitterness for long, because there was something deeply satisfying about seeing another woman at work in the house. To work again. To clean. To scrub. To have a purpose. People who depended on you. A proper family. Good things like Jack.

The Ghost Mother sighed and draped herself across Sarah's back. Overlaying her hands on top of the gloves, she followed her movements. Back and forth, fingers fully stretched. Then closer, her deadness tight against Sarah's shirt. Then even closer, brushing up against the small fair downy hairs above the skin of Sarah's neck.

Why not closer still? Easing herself down, the Ghost

Mother wrapped herself like a close-fitting cloak over the arch of Sarah's spine. Then under her hair, against her scalp. Lightly up against her cheek.

Direct contact with the skin.

And – this time – Sarah reacted. She jumped. For the first time she felt something graze her face. Automatically wiping her cheek to be rid of it, she laughed uncertainly, stood up and walked across the kitchen to put the kettle on. Get a grip, she thought, her hands shaking. All this ghost talk's spooked you. She even thought she could feel cool traces of air darting around her body, brushing against her like tiny winds.

Warm milk, she decided. No more coffee. One small cup before bed.

It was an accident. The Ghost Mother hadn't meant to touch Sarah's skin. She'd done it almost as a passing thought. But all that warmth tingling through her left the Ghost Mother feeling curiously moved.

Experimentally, she placed her face back against Sarah's. Then, as Sarah opened her mouth in surprise, the Ghost Mother slipped a spirit-finger past her lips.

This time Sarah gasped – a cooler essence touching her.

The Ghost Mother swiftly pushed her fingers even deeper inside Sarah's mouth.

Sarah breathed out heavily, and the Ghost Mother cursed as she was blown out into the corridor.

Inside his room, Jack coughed several times.

Sarah, her heart racing, listened, resisting an impulse to wake him. When she was satisfied the coughing fit had died down, she went back into the living-room, turning her shoulders this way and that. 'Don't be stupid,' she told herself, though even as she said it something made her jerk her head up to the nearest mirror.

The Ghost Mother floated next to Sarah's face. Could she get further inside? She'd never tried going inside living tissue before. Imagine all the extra strength she'd gain if she could actually take control! Strength to really work again. Strength to do anything. To become, for instance, Jack's mother.

The thought rose like a tantalizing, almost crushing hope.

Was it possible? If so, the beauty was that Jack need never know. She could pretend to be Sarah, at least until he was ready to hear the truth.

The Ghost Mother clenched her teeth, hardly able to contain her excitement. The other children had rejected her because she wasn't their true mother. But if she could do this . . .

Floating towards Sarah's mouth, she condensed her spirit body into its smallest size, determined to find a way past the lips. The mouth was a real barrier. Sarah's breath kept blowing her out before she could get far enough inside the throat to be safe from it. Circling her, the Ghost Mother searched for a way. She watched Sarah drinking her milk, making jittery twists and turns. She waited patiently until she calmed down, was quieter in her breathing, less likely to expel her.

From Jack's room, both women heard him cough again.

As Sarah lifted her head, the Ghost Mother squeezed against her lips. Then, wriggling her way inside, she felt a new presence drifting into the room.

Only one other spirit could have crept up on her so deftly.

'What are you doing?' Oliver shouted.

The Ghost Mother cursed and lashed out at him. 'Get out!' she demanded. 'This is none of your affair!'

He swayed away from her grasp. The Ghost Mother used the opportunity to steer herself towards Sarah's lips again.

From Oliver's position the breezes were light and tricky. Taking a risk, he let one of them carry him into the Ghost Mother. Slamming into her back, he knocked her away from Sarah.

'Leave us!' the Ghost Mother shrieked. 'Or I will take your soul!'

'Take it, then!'

Oliver challenged the Ghost Mother, risking himself. Every time she approached Sarah, he hit out at her. Then an unexpectedly strong current of air from the corridor picked him up and whirled him out of the room. 'Leave her alone!' he screamed, struggling in vain against it.

Sarah was standing near the mantelpiece when she felt something distinctly enter her. 'Jack?' she murmured, far too quietly for him to hear. Shivering, she put down her milk. She gazed around the room. She was suddenly aware of the chime of the grandfather clock, of wind rustling in the upper chimney.

A coldness gathered near her mouth. Sarah passed her hand across her face to brush it away, and, as she did so, she might have been aware of a shadowy weight, except that it was already so far inside her that there was no difference between her and that weight. Sarah blinked, and the weight was behind her eyes.

She shuddered. Felt a pressure. A movement. A will.

Twelve

A New, Fast Body

Oliver watched in horror as Sarah tried to regain control.

She jerked like a puppet, limbs twitching, her left arm fighting her right as each mother temporarily ruled different parts of her body. Then Sarah briefly wrestled control back and managed to get to the lounge door. She wrenched it open, tried to scream, to warn Jack, but her left hand slapped her mouth shut before any sound emerged. The same hand yanked her back inside the room.

For several minutes she lay on her side, half in and half out of the doorway, panting like a dog caught for too long in the sun.

Then the panting stopped. Her mouth relaxed and a small shiver ran down her legs. She propped herself up on one arm. Gingerly touching the tender part of her chin where it had been slapped, she slowly stood up. There was dust all over her skirt where she'd rolled around on the carpet. Carefully picking the dust particles off, she looked blearily around. It was what she did next, however, that made Oliver shudder. She looked at him – right at him – raised a single finger and crooked it, as if to reel him in. Then she gave him a spectacular smile, full of Sarah's white teeth.

'We have some old scores to settle, don't we?' she said knowingly. 'Let's see you get away from this new, fast body, Oliver. It won't be easy. The house breezes won't affect me any more. I'll give you a head start, shall I?'

Oliver swore and glided as fast as he could towards the doorway. The Ghost Mother let him go. She lay flat on her belly, resting her chin playfully in her hands, watching him leave, enjoying the anticipation of the chase.

Then she came after him.

From the physical struggle earlier, there was a breeze assisting Oliver through the lounge doorway, but little beyond it. Riding a cushion of barely rising air, using every manoeuvre he knew, Oliver made it to the staircase and ascended. The ceiling above him was the highest in the house.

Seeing where he was going, the Ghost Mother attempted to swipe him down before he could get too high, but he stayed just ahead of her. Shrieking, she ran for a chair. By the time she returned Oliver was high up against the landing ceiling, out of reach. The Ghost Mother folded her arms and nodded irritably.

'Well,' she said, 'I see I shall have to postpone my pleasure until later. But I'm afraid I cannot allow you to warn my new son about what has happened, Oliver. I could extract a promise from you not to tell him, but I doubt you'd honour it. I'll have to do something else to keep you quiet.' She cocked a hand to her ear. 'That's Gwyneth, counting too loudly again. I can always hear her. She never learns. They're in the kitchen, aren't they? I think I'll take my new body in there to show them.'

She strode across the corridor and kicked the kitchen door wide.

The ghost children were hidden, but as soon as the door opened Gwyneth screamed, giving her position away. Charlie stayed concealed beneath the fridge. Ann floated across the floor, trying to get to Gwyneth before the Ghost Mother, but there was no chance of that. With no breezes to contend with, the Ghost Mother ran straight across the room and picked Ann up. Holding her by the neck, she turned her effortlessly this way and that, testing out the strength of her new hands, making sure they didn't do any permanent damage.

Oliver floated back down the staircase.

'Stay away!' Ann told him. 'Oliver, there's no fighting her like this! Are you listening to me? You have to take care of Charlie and Gwyneth. They're your responsibility now. Are you listening?'

Oliver nodded in a stunned way, but Ann knew he was a fighter, not someone patient enough to look after the others. Charlie would follow him anywhere, but how would he cope with a frightened Gwyneth?

'If you hurt any of us, our agreement is over,' she told the Ghost Mother. 'I'll never co-operate with you again. Think about that.'

The Ghost Mother shrugged. 'I do not need your co-operation any more, Ann. I'll take whatever energy I require from your soul. Jack will give me everything else a mother needs.' She glanced at Oliver. 'If you tell him anything I will drain Ann completely. She won't survive that. Do you understand?'

'Don't listen to her!' Ann shouted. 'Tell Jack! You must –'

The Ghost Mother covered Ann's mouth. 'Oliver, if you say one syllable to Jack, I'll destroy her. Do you believe me?'

Oliver slowly nodded.

'Good. Then we understand each other.'

Tucking Ann under one arm, the Ghost Mother strolled out of the kitchen. It was the early hours of the morning, and very dark, as she made her way up the staircase. Once inside Sarah's bedroom, she spent a few moments studying Ann, deciding what to do with her. Then she opened the large wardrobe against the rear wall of the bedroom and placed Ann inside. 'I can't take any chances, I'm afraid. I'll have to lock you in.' Shutting the wardrobe door, she sealed the keyhole shut with masking tape, making sure there were no gaps. Then she went back downstairs and sat by the cold fireplace.

Oliver and the other children were gone, hiding somewhere, but the Ghost Mother suspected she could find them if she really tried. For now there were more important things to attend to. Preparing, for instance, for those first delicate and risky exchanges of conversation with Jack.

It was 01:45 a.m. and there was much to do to get ready for her new son. Starting with words. Her old style of conversation wouldn't convince anyone. Jack would know something was wrong straight away. It was necessary to speak like Sarah. Looking into her mind, the Ghost Mother plucked out the modern phrases she might need. Sarah fought to deny her every last one, of course, but the Ghost Mother was persistent.

'Let me out!' Sarah whispered.

'No, I'll not do that,' the Ghost Mother thought. 'I can't share Jack with you. I've waited too long for a chance like this. Stop fighting me. It'll be simpler that way. Give me what I need.'

'No.' Sarah screamed to break the Ghost Mother's concentration.

Ignoring the screams as best she could, the Ghost Mother took several sharp deep breaths – how wonderful to have a body that could breathe again! – and went into the kitchen. She'd seen people in the house using contemporary kitchen equipment, so she knew roughly how it all worked. However, she wanted to experiment fully with the oven, so that by morning she could manage it without awkwardness. After all, she would be using the oven a great deal. Jack was a growing boy. It was going to be a pleasure cooking for him. What were his favourite dishes? No idea, but never mind. Given enough time, she'd force Sarah to tell her all about them.

Opening the utensil drawer, the Ghost Mother ran a hand over one of the stainless steel spoons. In her own day, she'd scoured spoons with brick dust, the knives with emery paper, and the old cooking range had been a labour in itself, needing the hard graft of regular blackleading to prevent it rusting up. It was going to be so much easier being a mother now.

Once she was satisfied she knew her way around the kitchen, the Ghost Mother wandered around the other rooms. She checked complex devices like the telephone, recalling how Sarah had used it and how to disconnect it if she needed to. She made sure she was able to use the firelighters, so she and Jack could be cosy together beside a friendly fire. She played with the TV controls until she could deftly flick between the channels. Wandering into the bathroom, she applied a little of Sarah's deodorant. Easy to forget small details like that – getting the smells right. No doubt, in this hygienic age, Jack would be far more sensitive to odours than her own Isabella had been.

She tested out other bottles and hairsprays, then examined Sarah's toothbrush. In the Ghost Mother's own time a salted cloth had sufficed, but this thin-bristled object was obviously what Jack would expect her to use. She familiarized herself with it, brushing her teeth up and down, round and round, copying the way she'd seen Sarah doing it. Mm. Yes. Definitely better than a salted cloth. Smiling, she squeezed the spearmint toothpaste between her teeth.

After rinsing, she ambled back downstairs, humming a tune to herself. She made a hot drink. A cup of tea, no milk. It was the first taste that had passed her lips in over a hundred and fifty years, and she drank it down in slow sips, making it last, enjoying it immensely. Looking in the fridge, she saw that there were many other appetizing things to reacquaint herself with, or try for the first time. It was going to be interesting being a mother in this more affluent world.

Only one thing was wrong: she was tired. With Sarah

constantly fighting her to get back control, she was having to use a great deal of her soul energy. Well, perhaps that didn't matter. She'd take as much as she needed from Ann for the time being.

Selecting a ripe green apple, she carried it with her into the lounge. How was she going to get Jack to accept her? That was the big question. It wouldn't be easy. She had to come up with an explanation to account for any clumsiness on her part. As she bit through to the core of the apple, she glanced in the mirror and grinned, practising her smiles. It was important to find the right one for greeting Jack in the morning.

Thirteen

A Proper Little Man

Jack woke late again. He always felt drowsy in the days following an asthma attack, and generally slept for longer. Going into the bathroom, he was surprised to find the house quiet. His mum was usually up before him. She probably sat around most of the night listening out for me, he thought. Feeling guilty, and not wanting to wake her, he slipped quietly into the bathroom.

In the shower he had a good soak, knowing on past experience that the doctor would be giving him a thorough poke around. Afterwards, dressing in jeans and a T-shirt, he listened, but there was only silence from his mum's room. Must still be asleep, he thought. He decided to surprise her by making filter coffee and serving it to her in bed. She'd like that. And it would give him one more opportunity to talk her into staying in the house. Not much chance of success, but he had to try. He couldn't get the thought of the girl attached to the Ghost Mother's mouth out of his head.

Trudging down to the kitchen, he was looking for the coffee filters when he saw her. The door to the lounge was partially open, and she was perched on the edge of the sofa, like a visitor. She sat with a perfectly straight back, gazing vacantly at the ashes of the dead fire.

'Mum!' Jack said, going inside. 'You were quiet enough. I thought you were still in bed.'

The Ghost Mother's head jerked back. 'J-Jack!' A smile like a great gash of pride spread across her face. Sighing deeply, one hand on the arm of the sofa to steady herself, she rose, walked across the room and enfolded him deep in her arms.

'Hey, what's that for?'

She was reluctant to let him go. Finally, after a mild protest from Jack, she turned away, her face full of emotion.

Jack laughed to cover his embarrassment. 'Well, hey, good morning! I'll make some breakfast, eh?'

He switched the kettle on and popped four slices of bread in the toaster. The Ghost Mother stood behind him, watching his movements intently, saying nothing. As Jack spread jam on his toast, and took a bite, he glanced up at her.

'Mum, you look like you've never seen anyone eating a bit of bread before.'

'Is that always the way you prefer the jam?' she asked. 'From the fridge? Cold?'

'You know it is. What's the matter? You're looking a bit spooked.'

She offered him a brittle smile.

'Spooked? No, I . . . yes . . . yes, I am. I saw one of them.'

'A ghost?' Jack threw the toast down. 'You saw one! One of the ghost children, or –'

'No,' she said, hesitating. 'It was the Ghost Mother. Only briefly, but I spoke with her.'

'Where?'

'In here. This room. She floated in. She was angry about something – someone. A boy.'

'Oliver!' Jack cried. 'I told you! I told you they were here!'

'Yes, Jack. I doubted you. I didn't believe . . . I'm so sorry.' She smiled. 'Later I will help you look for them, but first, I am . . . not feeling too well. The shock –'

'I know! It was the same for me the first time!' Jack grinned, so happy she believed him at last that nothing else mattered. 'Do you need to go for a rest? It's OK, go on. Oh, Mum, this is great. You saw her, and –'

'Jack, please, I am not well.'

'Sorry. Here . . .' He helped guide her through the kitchen. 'You go and lie down. I'm all ready for the doctor, anyway. I'll wake you when he gets here. What time's he coming?'

'The doctor?'

'Yes.' Jack grinned. 'You know, the man who examines people. The doctor.'

'Oh yes. *Him*.' She said it with venom. 'Doctors, Jack. I've never trusted doctors. When you are truly ill what use are they? I have used' – she struggled to get the word out – 'the telephone to tell him that he will not be needed. I think it best if you just stay here and rest.'

'Really?' Jack stood by the kitchen table, stirring sugar into his tea. 'Mum, you're talking weirdly.'

'Am I?' She sighed. 'I'm sorry, Jack. Speaking with the Ghost Mother was a . . . strange experience.'

'I'll bet. So no doctor, then?'

'I think I can look after you far better than any doctor.'

Jack glanced up to see if she was joking. She didn't seem to be, but at that moment he didn't care.

'Mum, this is fantastic! You'll be miles better at talking to the Ghost Mother than me. You'll really be able to understand her, and –'

'I will do that, Jack. We won't leave now, at least until we can find and help the ghost children. But first, let me take a small rest . . .'

'Yeah, of course . . . of course. . .'

Jack helped her to the staircase. The Ghost Mother swept up it, suppressing a small grin of triumph.

Jack spent the next hour or so in his bedroom, waiting for one of the ghosts to visit him. When they didn't, he checked anxiously around the house, but couldn't find a trace. Where were they hiding? But he wasn't as worried as he had been. With his mum already talking to the Ghost Mother, he knew things could only improve. About mid-morning, after poking around a while in various places, calling Oliver's name, he took a break and went to fix himself a snack.

The Ghost Mother was already in the kitchen, waiting for him. She had decided to wear Sarah's longest skirt – all the trousers felt uncomfortable against her legs – and a blouse that covered her arms. As Jack entered, she stood at the sink, her back to him, preparing food. In her left hand there was a pear. As Jack watched she bit voraciously from it, a single bite, then put it down. Several other pieces of fruit and raw vegetables, all with one or two bites in them, were strewn across one side of the table.

In her right hand she held a five-inch-long carving knife. She was slowly chopping carrots with the knife, then clearing them with the side of her hand to the edge of the cutting board. It was an efficient method of cutting, though Jack had never seen her use it before. She hummed an odd tune to herself, one Jack didn't recognize. The table was set for lunch. Plates and cutlery were laid out, cups positioned neatly.

'What's up?' he asked. 'We having guests?'

She stopped and blinked at him. 'No, of course not.' She finished preparing the food. It was vegetable soup. Jack had had it before, but never tasting quite like this. 'Nice,' he said, helping himself to a second plateful.

The Ghost Mother watched him eat. It was a pleasure to see Jack enjoying her first attempt at a meal. But she was careful. She resisted the impulse to say anything unless he asked a direct question, because she kept tripping over the simplest of words – Sarah's constant shouting making it hard to focus. Instead, she let her taste buds, dormant for so long, linger over the food on her own plate. To eat again after all these years! She wanted to dwell over every spoonful, but was careful about that, too; she didn't want to draw attention to herself.

Jack didn't mention the packed bags sitting in the corner of the living-room. Although Sarah had said she'd help him find the ghosts, he wanted to keep any thoughts about leaving far from her mind. Instead, he went over everything he knew about the ghosts with her again, including his fruitless search this morning. He decided against mentioning Isabella yet, though – five ghosts were probably enough for his mum to cope with right now. The Ghost Mother listened closely, but her attention wandered whenever Jack mentioned the children, especially Oliver.

'Aren't you interested in him?' Jack asked, after a long silence.

'Yes.' She smiled.

'Oliver's scared of the Ghost Mother.'

No reaction. Just the smile.

'Are you listening, Mum?'

'Yes.' Her vague gaze was somewhere in the middle of his forehead. With a visible effort, she collected herself. 'And your . . . cough?' she asked. 'What of your cough? It seems less pronounced today.' Flustered, especially by all this admiring talk of Oliver, and with Sarah tormenting her in any way she could, the Ghost Mother sensed her control of language slipping. When Jack stared oddly at her she hurriedly cleared the table and asked him to retire with her to the lounge.

'Retire?'

'It's cool,' she said, biting her lip. 'Let's build the fire. After all, if there are ghosts in this house they may feel the chill as much as us.'

Listening to her talk, Jack realized how much the Ghost Mother had disturbed her. He wanted to sit his mum down, stay with her and make sure she was OK. They walked together into the lounge, but she made no move towards the fireplace. She just stared at Jack, that awkward smile perched on her face.

'I'll do it,' Jack said, wondering if he was meant to be taking a hint. 'I saw how you got the fire going yesterday.'

Under her watchful scrutiny he cleaned the fire out and arranged the firelighters. It took three matches to get a good blaze going. The closest radiator creaked as it expanded.

'You're a proper little man now,' she said suddenly. 'Aren't you?'

Jack wasn't sure how to reply to that.

'Mum, you're still behaving and talking a bit weirdly.'

'Come and sit closer to me.'

Jack pulled his chair up, just as he'd done on their first night together in the house. But the Ghost Mother wasn't content with how close he was; not until they were side by side and she could put her arm all the way around him did she seem satisfied.

They stared into the fire.

'This is getting to be a habit of ours,' Jack said, wanting to break the strange tension between them. 'See any shapes in the flames?'

'No.'

It was stifling in the room. The sun added to the heat, streaming through one of the windows. A bird called outside, a sad sound. Inside the grate of the fire a log shifted, sending sparks up the chimney.

'We're going to be so happy in this house,' the Ghost Mother said, tears brimming in her eyes. 'Jack, I feel that we are. Once these matters with the ghosts are dealt with, we are going to be so, so happy together here.'

*

In the afternoon they spent a couple of hours together unsuccessfully searching for the ghosts. The Ghost Mother made sure Jack searched especially well in places the children never went. The rest of the day passed uneventfully, with Jack increasingly concerned about not finding the ghost children, but also having no choice except to rest in his room, still recovering from the asthma scares of the past few days.

In the evening, after they'd eaten – a ready meal, the Ghost Mother wanted to cook something more elaborate, but why risk increasing Jack's suspicions? – she said she would be pleased if he spent a little more time with her by the hearth.

She sat close to him on the sofa until night settled in. The fire was stiflingly hot, and by the time Jack finally managed to extricate himself from her embrace he could barely stop yawning. He said goodnight, she kissed him – on the forehead, the way Sarah did it – and Jack traipsed upstairs. Too tired even to clean his teeth properly, he undressed, got straight into bed and pulled the duvet up to his neck. His last thought before he fell asleep was that more than anything else in the world he wanted to know what had happened to the red-haired girl in the white slip.

Fourteen

Ringlety-Jing

Ann's body, deep inside Sarah's wardrobe, felt cold. She couldn't stop shivering. It was only when a numbness started creeping over her heels that she understood why – her soul was fading; almost all its energy was gone. The Ghost Mother's last draught had taken nearly the last of it, and the Nightmare Passage's long wait for her soul was almost over.

There was virtually no air left inside the wardrobe to float on. Ann could barely find enough to lift her head. Not that it mattered. There was no reason to lift her head anyway. The wardrobe offered no view of the bedroom – the keyhole was sealed with masking tape.

Resting against one of Sarah's denim jackets, Ann waited for the Nightmare Passage to claim her. There was nothing she could do to stop that now. But she still had one hope: that the Nightmare Passage would take her before the

Ghost Mother drained the last of her soul. It would be good to deny her that, at any rate. And alongside this hope was another: that Oliver wouldn't find her in time. She knew he'd attempt to rescue her. But for all his fighting spirit he'd be no match for a Ghost Mother armed with Sarah's body. And if she caught Oliver now, Ann realized, the Ghost Mother wouldn't hold back. She'd waited too long for that. She would gorge on his soul until nothing remained except the husk the Nightmare Passage takes for itself. The thought of Oliver's bright soul being at the mercy of that desolate place filled Ann with despair.

Could she help him? Could she at least speed up her journey into the Nightmare Passage so he had no reason to look for her? Her feet were tucked underneath her, wrapped in the cotton slip to ward off the chill. Stretching them out, Ann deliberately exposed them again. She let the cold seep into her legs, and prayed for the darkness of the Nightmare Passage to overwhelm her.

'You have to!' Oliver growled. 'Gwyneth, just do it!'

'No!'

'What do you mean, no? Do you know how dangerous it is for us to be out here? Stop dithering and just get inside! Do I have to beg? Is that what you want? You want me on my knees? What's the matter with you? Charlie, tell her!'

The three of them were squeezed inside a narrow gap between planks under the larder floor. Many years before Ann had chosen a location for each of them to hide in an emergency. The locations were meant to be secret even from each other, so that if they were found the Ghost Mother couldn't scare them into revealing the hideouts of the others. But Gwyneth wouldn't go to hers without Ann to coax her. She'd insisted Charlie hold her hand the whole way, and now they were there she refused to stay inside.

'I won't,' she whimpered. 'It's too dark.'

'Look, just get in there!' Oliver demanded.

'You can't make me!'

'If Ann told you to, you'd do it fast enough!'

'Stop shouting!'

'I'll stop shouting if you do what you're told!'

Oliver knew he'd spoiled any chance of gaining Gwyneth's willing co-operation. He'd rushed and jostled her through the risky parts of the house. When she'd stopped right in the middle of the corridor to cry over the loss of Ann, his patience had snapped altogether and he'd forcibly dragged her here. Stupid, he realized. Really dumb. He knew she'd prefer to be with Ann now, locked away somewhere, anywhere, rather than here with him. And her mood wasn't improved by the discovery of fresh mouse droppings at her secret location, either. She kept looking round for more of them.

'It's horrible!' she wailed. 'It's . . . it's dirty!'

'Nah, it's OK,' Oliver muttered, getting Charlie to nod along with him. 'Just a mouse run. Think of it as company. With all your crying they'll never come back, anyway.'

'You stay here then!'

She stared at him, her lower lip trembling.

'I'll sing you a song,' Charlie piped up, trying to keep the peace.

'Yeah,' Oliver said. 'How about that, Gwyneth? A nice song. We'll both sing it.'

She sniffed, surprised by the offer. Oliver always

mocked the rhymes Ann sang her. 'Will you?'

'No problem,' Oliver said. 'Listen, Gwyneth, I'll even stand on my head and warble if you like, but if I do you'd better let me and Charlie go to our own secret locations.' He managed a smile.

'No, you'll muck up the words. You'll spoil it! You always do! You'll mess it up!'

'We'll both sing it properly, OK? Nicely. Try anyway.' Oliver took a deep breath, glanced sheepishly at Charlie, and began, 'The waves of a mighty sorrow –'

'Not that one,' Gwyneth said.

'What then?'

'The Ringlety-jing one.'

'I can't sing that. It's stupid! I don't even know the words . . .' Oliver saw the stubborn look on her face, sighed and gathered himself.

'Ringlety-jing!' he muttered tonelessly. 'Ringlety –'

'Sing it the same way Ann does.'

'Don't be an idiot. I haven't got a girl's voice!' Gwyneth's lower lip wobbled. 'OK. OK.' Oliver cleared his throat. 'Ringletyyyyyy-jing! Ringletyyyyy-jing! Ringlettyyy-jing-jing! And what shall we sing? Some little crinkety-crakety thing, that rhymes and – aggh!' He cursed, unable to remember the rest.

'It's all right,' Charlie said. He shut his eyes to help him recall the way the rhyme went. It wasn't one of those Ann often sang:

> *'Ringlety-jing!*
> *And what shall we sing?*
> *Some little crinkety-crankety thing*

> *That rhymes and chimes*
> *And skips, sometimes,*
> *As though wound up with a kink*
>   *in the spring.'*

Charlie finished. Having sung the whole verse perfectly, he turned to Oliver. 'I'll look after Gwyneth,' he said. 'She won't stay here on her own anyway. She's too scared. I'll stay with her.'

Oliver studied him closely. 'Are you sure?'

'Yes.'

'You really think you can keep her quiet?'

'If Charlie stays with me I *will* be quiet,' Gwyneth said.

Will you now? Oliver thought. What if the lovely Ghost Mother comes after you? How quiet will you be then?

'I promise,' Gwyneth told him.

Charlie gazed up. 'You're not going to your secret location anyway, are you, Oliver? You're off to warn Jack. You shouldn't.'

'It's what Ann wanted.'

'It's too risky.'

'Then I'll just have to be careful, won't I?' Oliver sighed. 'Look, I can't just hide, Charlie. What if that was your mum out there? Anyway, if I don't get a message to him, who will? You? Gwyneth?'

'I . . . I can try,' Charlie said.

But they all knew the Ghost Mother would find Charlie long before he could get anywhere near Jack. Only Oliver was fast enough to evade her, and now even he might not be.

'She'll be waiting for you,' Charlie said.

Oliver shrugged. 'So what? I'm not letting her scare me witless just because she's got a whole new body to play with. She'll be able to move faster, but she can't squeeze inside cracks any more like us, can she? And she'll be noisier, too. I'm bound to hear her big feet a mile off.'

'What if she catches you?'

Oliver grunted. 'She's never seen anything like the fight I'll put up if she does. Even if she gets hold of me, it won't be the end, I guarantee you that.' Bending down, he whispered in Charlie's ear, 'You're asking a lot of yourself, taking charge of Gwyneth. It's a brave move, but are you sure? Do you really think you can keep her quiet if old Weepy turns up?'

Charlie grinned. 'I can keep her quieter than you, anyway.'

Oliver grinned back. 'That's true. I was never cut out to be much of a mother, was I?'

'No, you're rubbish at it.'

Oliver laughed. 'Well put. Now listen, and see if you agree with me. I think I'm going to go after Ann first. If Weepy's got her tucked away somewhere, she's bound to get hungry sometime soon and remember she's got a nice soul-meal ready and waiting. We can't let that happen without doing something about it. Probably not much chance of helping Ann escape, but I have to try. If I meet Jack on the way and can get him a message, fine, I'll do it. But Ann first.'

Charlie nodded and so did Gwyneth.

'Yes,' she said. 'Find Ann. We'll wait for you, and I'll be good.'

Oliver gave her a look. 'You'll be quiet? You won't count out loud, and give Charlie away?'

'No.'

'Promise?'

'I promise.'

'Even if the mice come back?'

She nodded.

Oliver chewed his lip, turned to Charlie and murmured, 'You don't have to do this just to impress me, you know.'

'I know.'

'Are you sure?'

'Yes.'

Oliver winked at Charlie and gave Gwyneth a stern look. 'I need you to do one more thing for me, Gwynnie. Charlie boy here isn't very keen on the dark. It scares him. He's gonna need his hand holding a hell of a lot. He probably wants it held all the time. I want you to look after him for me, make sure he's OK. Think you can do that?'

Gwyneth gave him a puzzled nod and squeezed Charlie's hand. Oliver glanced once into the scullery to make sure the Ghost Mother was not there, offered Charlie a final grin and rode a wisp of air into the main part of the house.

Fifteen

I'm a Good Mother, Aren't I?

In her new body, unaffected by the breezes of the house, the Ghost Mother slept long and soundly. Even Sarah's shrieks did not keep her awake for long. She slept, and woke well rested and ready for her second morning with Jack.

Yesterday she'd made many mistakes. However, the evening had ended cosily enough, nestled up against Jack's thigh by the fire. And though modern words still felt peculiar on her tongue, she was beginning to master their sounds. Sarah, screaming to get out, was, after all, teaching her more and more of them.

The Ghost Mother decided on an early start. A few deep breaths to wake her, then up and about in Sarah's room, testing out her clothes, searching for something sensible to wear. There were none of the embellishments, ribbons or curl-papers of her own time, but even so there were still plenty of ways to get up her best looks. Nothing too fancy, of course. She experimented with applying Sarah's pink lipstick, foundation cream and mascara, and using the hair curlers. The results were hideous.

'Help me,' she whispered. 'I'm not used to doing this.'

From inside her, Sarah answered, 'Don't you understand? I'll make it harder, not easier. I won't let you rest. I'll fight you for everything.'

'He's my son now.'

'No. You can't force a child to love you. If you let me out –'

'Let you out? I'll never let you out,' the Ghost Mother said. 'Not now. Not ever. Not unless Jack is dead. And if that happens, you won't want to be let out. You'll wish you were dead as well. You'll wish you were as dead as me.'

Sarah searched for a reply to that.

'What happened to you?' she asked at last. 'How did you become so bitter?' She knew there had to be a way to break through the Ghost Mother's defences. She'd already looked inside much of her mind. Horrors lurked there, though the Ghost Mother hid the worst of them from her.

'You had a daughter who loved you once,' she said. 'Tell me about that. What really happened to her? She didn't just die of consumption, did she?'

No reply.

'What are you hiding? Did you do something to her?'

The Ghost Mother held her breath.

'What did you do?'

'Be quiet.'

'Did you . . . did you kill her?'

Total silence.

'Oh, so that's it. You killed her. Oh, you did, didn't you? You killed Isabella. You killed your own daughter.'

The Ghost Mother silently screamed. 'That's what you want, isn't it?' she hissed. 'For Jack to see me like this – wild, out of control.'

'Yes. The way you really are. Why did you kill Isabella?'

'Leave me alone!'

'There is no worse crime for a mother than that,' Sarah murmured. 'Oh, and she loved you, didn't she? Isabella loved you very much.'

'No. I . . . I *did not* kill her!'

'No? Then why the guilt? I think you did. I wonder if Isabella blamed you? Do you think so? In those final moments, before she died, do you think she hated you as much as Oliver does now? As much as all the ghost children do? As much as Jack will?'

'Stop your mouth!' the Ghost Mother wailed.

'Is it because you killed Isabella that you've found it easier to take the souls of so many other children? Did one death make it easier?'

'I was lonely. The Nightmare Passage . . . I never meant –'

'To harm them? I see. So that is your excuse. Isabella, I think, would have been so proud of you for that.'

The Ghost Mother clenched her fists, fighting down the nausea threatening to overwhelm her. Ignoring Sarah as best she could, she finally managed to fill her mind again with loving thoughts about Jack. I will not harm him, she thought. I will love him, and he will love me.

Staring at her reflection in the mirror, she decided that

she hated the make-up. Jack will have to get used to you as you are sooner or later, she thought. Take it all off. If he queries anything, say you are ill. Yes, if anything goes wrong today, just tell him you are ill. Blame the ghosts; they've frazzled your nerves. He'll accept that.

She permitted herself a small smile. It was good to think about Jack, to behave like a real mother again. True, her mind kept wandering away from the present, but she'd make up for any minor forgetfulnesses and mistakes by smothering Jack with love. Not that she would expect too much from him in return. Not yet. Just sitting with him by the fire was enough for now. Later, perhaps, she might dare to hope that he'd regard her with some measure of genuine affection.

Should she dress to impress him? No. Nothing showy. Just be natural, she thought. Laugh if he makes a joke. Show an interest in whatever he does. Compliment him. Let him know that you have a sense of humour.

Wiping the make-up off her face, the Ghost Mother grinned into the mirror. No mistakes today, she thought. The toast. The tea. Get them right. Jack likes his breakfast just so.

As soon as Jack woke that morning, thoughts of Oliver and Ann flashed straight into his mind. I'm going to find you both today, he decided. I won't stop searching until I do.

Downstairs, the Ghost Mother was waiting for him, armed with a radiant smile. Jack noticed a tiny smudge of pink lipstick at the side of her mouth. Her hair looked as if it had been curled, then slept on.

'Going out somewhere?' he asked.

The smile faded, and she shook her head.

The breakfast table was set immaculately. There were four slices of toast on Jack's plate, each with a perfectly burned edge. A spreading knife gleamed beside the jam. His cup of tea was nice and hot and sugared just right. While he sipped it, the Ghost Mother also poured herself a cup from the pot.

'Tea?' Jack said. 'When did you start drinking that, Mum?'

She hesitated. 'I . . . wanted a change.'

'But you hate tea. You've always hated it.'

'No need to be so bold.'

'Bold? What does that mean?'

When she did not answer, Jack felt the tension suddenly rise between them.

He glanced away. A faint smell of more burning drew his attention to the bin. Six blackened slices of bread stuck out, ones she'd obviously overdone before he came down. There was also a slightly stale, musty smell coming from the bin itself – yesterday's old food leftovers hadn't been thrown out. The kitchen blinds were still closed as well. An apple core, at least a day old, festered on the work top.

With Sarah muttering destructively in her ear, the Ghost Mother turned to the sink. She picked up the nearest utensil – a bread knife – and set about rapidly peeling potatoes. She cut her finger almost immediately, but did not cry out, hoping Jack wouldn't notice. The blood ran from her finger onto the potato peelings.

'Mum, are you OK?'

She turned to him, smiled and wiped the blood on her apron.

133

'It's nothing.'

'No, it's a bad cut. Let me see.'

She snatched her hand away when he went to touch her – she didn't want him learning any truths that way.

'Hey!' he protested. 'I was only trying to help. What's the matter?'

She left the bleeding finger under the cold tap for a minute, then wrapped it in a kitchen towel.

'Mum,' Jack said, wanting to reach out to her in some way through all this awkwardness. 'What's the matter? Are you all right? You're not, are you?'

'What is wrong exactly? What am I doing wr–' She twisted away. 'No,' she said, trying to smile. 'I'm . . . not well, nor have I been for days. All these sightings of the ghosts, and the way the Ghost Mother talked. I've tried to hide the strain I'm under, but you can see it. Of course you can. You're my son.'

As she stepped towards him, Jack saw a puff of foundation cream on the lobe of one of her ears. She also smelled faintly. Hadn't she washed? What was wrong with her?

'I'm a good mother, aren't I?' she suddenly burst out.

'Of course you are!' Jack answered. 'Mum, don't be stupid, of course you are!'

She stood there, a few tears misting her eyes, nodding at him.

'I'll go look for the ghost children on my own,' he said. 'You don't have to get involved if it bothers you. It's OK.'

'Oh, Jack, I really don't think we should trouble ourselves about the ghost children any longer.' The Ghost Mother straightened up, the tears gone instantly. 'It has been some time since you saw them, after all. If they wish to contact us, they can. Hunting for them could be dangerous.'

'Is that what the Ghost Mother told you?'

'Yes.'

'Mum, we can't believe her. The girl –'

'Must we continue to discuss this? Have you seen the ghosts recently? Have you? Well?'

'No.'

'So why do we need to keep looking for them? I don't understand. What is the matter with you?'

'What's the matter with *me*? Mum it's you –'

'Jack, enough!' The Ghost Mother stabbed the knife into the bread board. 'Must you query every remark of mine? Is it too much to ask that you do not do so? Is that really too much for your mother to ask? To expect a little peace and tranquillity in this house?'

'No. No . . . Of course not.'

Jack said it automatically, too amazed by her outburst to think of anything else. He half expected her to break out laughing, to show she was joking. Instead, she gazed solemnly at him. Jack looked at her hands. The nails on most of her fingers were bitten almost to the quick. When she caught him staring, she hid them.

'Eat up,' she said brightly. 'A good breakfast keeps up your strength. Isn't this what you like?' She turned away from him, sipping her tea. No milk, he noticed. He'd never seen her drink anything hot without milk. Standing up from the table, he backed away from her.

'I'd like to go to my room,' he said.

'Why?' Instantly suspicion on her face.

'To play a PC game, that's all. Something wrong with that?'

'No . . . of course you may. Very well. Yes, that's fine. Go to your room if you're finished eating. I'm not keeping you here. Go and play.'

For a while, stomach churning, Jack sat in his room just trying to understand what was happening. *Go and play!* He could hardly believe she'd said that. What on earth was wrong with her? He wanted to phone someone, maybe their doctor, but his mobile wasn't working for some reason. He'd have to use the main telephone in the lounge. He didn't want to do that, because his mum was bound to be in there.

I'm scared of her, he realized. How can I be scared of her?

Was she annoyed with him about something he'd done? That's ridiculous, he thought. Even so, he felt an unusually strong impulse to tidy up his room, just in case she came in and found fault with it.

He was still reeling, attempting to make sense of it all, when she knocked on his door.

'Come in,' he said thickly.

She stood there, smiling away from the threshold.

'I'm sorry, Jack. Sorry I shouted at you. This farmhouse . . . the ghosts –' she pulled a face '– it's made me really jittery. I shouldn't have scolded you like that. The important thing is that we're together. Nothing else matters.'

She served up lunch shortly afterwards. Some kind of meat dish, with boiled cabbage and potatoes. Jack had no idea what it was. He didn't ask because he wasn't in the mood for unnecessary conversations. She also seemed content for them to sit together without talking.

'You're very quiet,' she said at one point during the meal.

'So are you.'

'Just so. It is not necessary to talk all the time, is it?'

'No.'

'We can sit here and be happy just doing that, can't we?'

'Yes.'

He picked up a magazine and pretended to be doing a crossword so he could avoid her constant, unnerving gaze.

'Show me,' the Ghost Mother said.

'You're not normally interested in crosswords.'

'Of course I'm interested. I'm interested in everything you do, Jack.'

'Here.' Jack shoved the magazine over. 'I'm going back to my room.'

As soon as he left, the Ghost Mother slumped down in one of the kitchen chairs. What a disastrous morning! One foolish blunder after another! If the afternoon went as badly, Jack was bound to discover the truth. That mustn't happen. *It's your fault*, she thought, turning her attention inward to Sarah. Why won't you leave me alone? Why won't you stop screaming?

There had to be a way to prevent Sarah's endless interference. In fact, if she had more soul-energy to fight her with, perhaps Sarah's resistance could be overcome once and for all. The Ghost Mother considered where she could find a lot more energy, a great burst of it.

Of course.

She checked first in all the usual places for the ghost children, but Oliver had concealed their tracks well. No matter; one of them, at least, had nowhere to hide. She strolled upstairs to Sarah's bedroom. Once inside, she reached up to a shelf for the pretty bronze key that opened the wardrobe.

Ann prepared herself. Hearing the Ghost Mother quietly crossing the room, she sat up as best she could. There was a soft rasp as the masking tape was removed from the keyhole, followed by sunlight. Then she saw the Ghost Mother's eye, filling the space, making sure she was still there.

All day Ann had encouraged the Nightmare Passage to take her, dreading the arrival of this moment. When the Nightmare Passage did not take her, she had rehearsed over and over the arguments she would use to save herself, to persuade the Ghost Mother not to do this. But when that hungry eye appeared in the keyhole, and the Ghost Mother stood there tapping the key impatiently against her palm, Ann knew in her heart that nothing she said would make any difference.

Stay away, Oliver, she thought. Please, whatever happens, don't interfere now.

The Ghost Mother refused to meet her stare.

'If you are going to take the rest of my soul, look at me,' Ann dared her. 'At least do that.'

The Ghost Mother held the key rigid in her hands. There was no yielding in her gaze, no late spark of compassion.

'Do you want to know,' Ann whispered, 'what the Nightmare Passage feels like when you are this close to it?'

The Ghost Mother said nothing.

'No? You don't wish to hear? You coward. Now you are sending me into it, I didn't think you would.'

'If there was another way . . .'

'There is. Give me back some of the energy you've stolen over the years.'

'No.' The Ghost Mother reached into the wardrobe and lifted Ann's body off the clothes. She picked her up gently, the way a daughter might be lifted, and Ann couldn't help a sudden, desperate hope that she would stop. But then the Ghost Mother tilted her face in the disgusting way Ann knew only too well.

'It won't hurt,' the Ghost Mother promised. 'I'll make it swift.'

'You were a good mother once,' Ann pleaded. 'You were. When you sent Daniel into the Nightmare Passage it was an accident. I know it was. You never meant for it to happen. But this time you know what will happen to me. Please don't send me there.'

'I have no choice.'

'You have. Help me instead.'

The Ghost Mother lifted Ann towards her face. When Ann resisted, she forced her lips wide. Then the Ghost Mother bent down, and the gesture was like that of a kiss being offered, but of course it was nothing like a kiss.

This time, however, Ann's eyes did not widen with the usual horror.

At first the Ghost Mother did not understand what was wrong. She kept pressing herself closer, changing her grip on Ann's face, aware that barely a trace of soul was entering her throat. Then she detached herself.

Ann smiled triumphantly. 'Can't find anything? That's because I've nothing left to give. You've already taken it all.'

'No!' the Ghost Mother wailed. She clutched Ann, trying to force her lips to offer up more. Then she screamed with pain and dropped her, because suddenly Ann was too cold to hold.

Something terrifying had invaded the room.

Shrieking, the Ghost Mother hauled herself away, weeping with fear for her own safety.

Ann's face darkened. Ice crystals formed in her throat. Her hair froze.

The Nightmare Passage was here to snatch her away at last.

Over recent hours, Ann had longed for this. She had even begged the Nightmare Passage to take her. But now the moment had come, she couldn't help herself; she resisted it. Like every soul that had been claimed before her, with whatever strength she still had left, she fought its pull, holding desperately on to this world.

For a few seconds she was successful. The lower part of her body was wrenched away, but her upper half remained in the wardrobe, illuminated by sunshine. While it was still there, Ann reached out blindly to anyone, even the Ghost Mother, for help.

And found, instead – Oliver.

He'd arrived in the room in time to clutch one of her arms.

'Get away!' Ann screamed.

But it was too late. The Ghost Mother saw him. She lunged, and seized Oliver from the air.

Ann had never seen anything like the way Oliver fought her. His nails tore at her cheeks. His fingers gouged her eyes. His legs kicked out, striking her time and again. But soon the Ghost Mother found his face, and attached herself. Then her lips sought his, making a seal, and after that Oliver's legs kicked less. His hands continued to scratch her for a time, but gradually they fell limp as well, until finally even his neck slumped. It slumped so low that the Ghost Mother had to reach down to hold it up to stay attached to his face.

The last thing Ann saw before the Nightmare Passage stole her from this world was the Ghost Mother stop to take a breath, obscenely wipe her hand across her mouth, then turn back to Oliver for more.

Sixteen

A Mother Who Is Not a Mother

When Jack returned downstairs that afternoon the blinds were still closed, the apple core still festering on the work top. There was even a fresh whiff of burnt bread hanging in the air. More attempts to get the toast right, he thought. What's the matter with her?

She's ill. She told you herself. That's all it is. She's ill.

He desperately wanted to believe that.

The Ghost Mother stood at the cooker, stirring yet another pan of food Jack did not recognize.

'Did you enjoy your time alone, son?'

As she twisted towards him, Jack saw foundation cream *still* on her earlobe. A cursory glance in the mirror and she'd have spotted it. How could she have missed something so obvious? Perhaps it was that – the badly applied make-up. Or perhaps it was the state of the kitchen. Maybe it was the false smile, or the burnt toast, just way too much burning. Whatever it was, Jack knew that nothing was right about this. It was all wrong.

Part of him wanted to get his mum to hospital. The other part wanted to flee.

'I've seen the ghost children again,' he lied, watching her reaction closely. 'I've seen Oliver. I like Oliver. I like him a lot.'

The Ghost Mother stirred the pan.

'Don't ignore me,' Jack said.

'I'm not ignoring you.'

'Yes, you are. You don't like hearing about Oliver, do you? Not one bit.'

Her body, poised over the sink, tensed.

'Jack,' she said, in a deliberate, controlled tone, 'I am trying to make a home for us here. I am trying, yet you continue to be ungrateful. I can tell you are lying about seeing Oliver. I am prepared to indulge many things, but not lies. It upsets me to hear them from my own son. I do not like to see you lying, and I do not wish to have to punish you.'

Jack's heart thudded. He took a puff from his inhaler, restraining an impulse to run.

The Ghost Mother stared at him uncertainly.

'There are indications,' she said, 'that the weather will be fine later. Perhaps the outside air will alleviate your lungs.'

Her smile could not have been falser.

Only one person I know talks like that, Jack thought.

Not my mother. It came like a quick stab, and he tried to deny it, but couldn't. Not my mother. Not my mother.

I know who you are! The whole of him wanted to scream it out loud, but the horror of what it meant held him back.

Because if it was true, where was his real mum?

He had to be sure. How do you test if your mother is truely your mother?

She sat there, watching him. She didn't speak, didn't offer him any more clues, merely studied him, her hands squirming in her lap.

'Is it a relief not to talk?' Jack asked. 'It must be. That way you make fewer mistakes, don't you?'

She said nothing.

'Mum?' he whispered. 'Mum, are you in there? Can you hear me?'

He watched the smile slip, followed by a grimace. Then the smile clicked smoothly back into place.

'Too late,' Jack said quietly. 'I saw.'

The Ghost Mother wailed with frustration, her head suddenly jerking to the left.

'GET OUT!' his real mother's voice screamed from her. 'JACK, ANY WAY YOU CAN, GET OUT OF –'

The head whipped back into place.

'I . . . I . . . always wanted a son,' the Ghost Mother stuttered, trying to recover. 'I always . . . always . . .' She took a step towards Jack, but he backed away. 'Please,' she pleaded. 'Why won't you love me?'

The words made Jack spin. They hung in the air like a direct challenge. Love her! How could she expect that? She gazed at him, her expression full of need. What should he do until he could get away? Play the part of the dutiful son? Pretend? Is that what she expected?

'Is it so hard to care for me, Jack? Is it?'

'You're not my mother!' The words came out in a hoarse rasp. 'Not my real mother. I know you're not. How can I love you? Not my mother! Not my mother!'

Her eyes locked with his.

'Where is she?' Jack yelled. 'What have you done to her?'

The Ghost Mother sighed and strolled into the lounge. She lay on the sofa and gazed at a wall.

Jack stayed where he was, his breathing a mess. Then he took a deep lungful of air and walked into the lounge, prepared to bolt if she moved a step towards him. The Ghost Mother was positioned lengthways across the sofa, her legs drawn up, hugging herself. When she picked at the collar of her shirt, a speck of foundation cream flicked onto her neck.

Jack seethed with rage as she wiped it off with her hand.

'You're wearing her clothes! You're wearing her make-up! Take them off!'

The Ghost Mother gazed back at him serenely.

'I want her back!' Jack screamed.

'Do you truly and honestly want her back, Jack?'

'Yes!'

'Well, I am not surprised.' She sounded disappointed in him. 'We all have only one mother, and must unfortunately make do with that and grasp what love we can. You are only a boy, Jack, and do not understand everything. I cannot countenance allowing her back when I can bring you at least as much love as her. More love, in fact.'

'What?'

'If you give me a chance, I will be a more loving mother

to you than she ever was.'

Jack stared at her. 'If you love me, if you mean that, bring her back now.'

The Ghost Mother paused, licking her lips. 'Very well. I will.' Her face convulsed, then relaxed, and when she next looked up again it was with a milder expression.

'Jack? Jack, is that you?'

He leaned towards her, but the second her lips made contact with his cheek he drew back. He could tell it wasn't his mum who'd kissed him. He knew it was the Ghost Mother, and all ideas of pretending to be the dutiful son left his mind.

Stepping away from her, he rubbed his hand dismissively across his cheek, and made sure she saw him do it.

The Ghost Mother blinked uncertainly. 'There. I have given you what you wanted. Given you . . . your mother. Any time you want her again, I will return Sarah to you . . . as I have just done. Do you see how good I am to you, Jack? I'm your mother. I won't ever allow anything to harm you.'

Jack said, 'That wasn't my mum. Anyway, you're lying. How can you take care of me when you couldn't even take care of your own daughter?'

He had no idea what reaction he'd get to that, but he knew the words would get some response, and they did.

Her mouth dropped open. 'How could you . . .'

'I've seen her!' Jack said. 'Here, in this house. Isabella! I've talked to her!'

'You have not!' Instantly furious, the Ghost Mother lunged towards him. Jack hit out at her, but she flipped him onto his back and stood over his chest. 'How dare you mention her in such a casual way, playing frivolous games with me! Her name is mine alone to call upon in my periods of private grief!'

'She's alive! No, not alive, but she's –'

The Ghost Mother put her hand across his mouth. 'She is not! She is not! I have been in this house for years. Do you think I would have missed any sign?' Her face was white with anger. 'My daughter is gone. Dead. Dead.' She dragged Jack out of the lounge. When he tried speaking again she raised her arm as if to strike him. 'Enough!' she screamed. 'I am in earnest!' Seizing his collar, she hauled him along the corridor.

Jack fought her, but stopped when his breathing became tight.

'Where . . . are you taking me?'

She lugged him up the staircase and onto the landing. Pushing him into his bedroom, she dumped him on the floor.

'You will stay here!' she screamed. 'In your room. . . until . . . until you learn to behave like a proper son! I will not tolerate this kind of behaviour! Do you hear me? Are these the manners you were taught? Is this the behaviour your own mother allowed?' She glanced at the rocking chair. 'And I shall take *this* back!' She yanked the chair up and carried it into Isabella's old room. When she returned, she announced, 'Jack, there is only one requirement I have of you at this moment, and that is patience. I ask at least a modicum of that, and I do not think I ask too much. It is not easy for me to be a mother in this strange new world. But I am trying.' She beat her breast passionately. 'I am

147

trying my heart out! A little patience, and tender enough mercy upon my soul not to reject me before you even know me. Is that so much to ask?'

Jack thought about pushing past her, then changed his mind. If he tried to run from the farmhouse, who knew what she'd do? He couldn't outrun her anyway. Running would only set off another asthma attack. There was a better way. Use the phone. 999. Report a burglary, or murder. Anything to get the police to the house.

'I think I have reason to believe I can be a better mother than yours ever was,' the Ghost Mother told him, calming down slightly. 'Let us speak no further on this subject now. We are both weary, and you need to rest. I request only one thing for the present: stay in your room, Jack. That is all I ask.'

What does she want to hear? he thought. I've got to get her to trust me for long enough to make that phone call.

'I'll give you time,' he muttered. 'I'll give you time to prove you can be a mother. But I have a condition.'

She gazed at him warily. 'Well?'

'You have to give me longer to get used to you, without expecting too much in return. I'm just . . . it's . . . it's difficult for me.'

She nodded – surprised, grateful.

'In the meantime,' Jack reassured her, 'I won't leave you. I won't leave the house.' He saw her doubting look. 'I promise.'

'Thank you, Jack. Thank . . .' A huge pent-up welling of emotion shot up in the Ghost Mother's chest, and she fell to her knees in front of him. 'Oh Jack, thank you. Thank you. Thank you so much!' She stayed like that on the floor, and when she rose again it was as if a great weight were lifting from her.

'And since we are being honest with one another,' she noted, looking down with disdain at her clothing, 'I will be honest also, and remove these garments. You are right: they are your mother's, and do not look appropriate on me. I am a woman of plainer tastes, as you will discover, Jack. I make this additional promise to you also. I will not ask you to love me. There. That is hard for a mother to say, but I will not ask it. Not until you are ready.'

She left and swept across the landing to Sarah's bed-room.

Jack remained where he was. Several times he thought of scurrying downstairs, but it was too risky. Who knew what reaction the Ghost Mother would have if she saw him holding the phone?

She soon returned, knocking timidly on his bedroom door. As she stepped inside, Jack saw that she'd scrubbed off any last touches of make-up. She'd also changed into Sarah's simplest dress – a plain dark brown one. 'Until I can find more appropriate attire, I have to wear some-thing,' she said apologetically. Her hair was tied back in a severe bun. 'Suitably different from Sarah's,' she said, fixing it in position with a few steel grips. 'If, that is, you approve this look?'

Jack nodded, wanting to scream, but managing to keep a neutral expression on his face.

It began raining outside, a light pitter-patter.

They both listened.

'I will not keep you here, comparing the differences between Sarah and me,' the Ghost Mother said brightly.

The anxious smile was gone. She was in complete control again now. 'You may stay in your room, Jack. Rest your chest awhile, and take some time to consider what we have discussed. And consider also the promises we have made solemnly to one another.'

She closed his door. He heard her tramp downstairs. Shortly after, she came back upstairs, her feet crossing the landing. Heading towards Isabella's room, he realized. Of course. Where else would she go? He soon noticed the unmistakable creak of the rocking chair on the floorboards.

For the rest of the afternoon Jack remained in his room, hoping for an opportunity to use the phone. He decided to delay until she went to the bathroom. The wait was interminable, but at last she did, and he slipped downstairs. When he picked up the phone receiver there was no dialling tone. The line was dead. Following the connecting wires, he saw where the Ghost Mother had pulled them out of the wall. He checked all the windows in the lounge and dining room. They wouldn't budge — painted shut. He'd forgotten about that. Hurrying back upstairs, he barely made it to his bedroom before the Ghost Mother made sure he was inside. She gave him a frozen smile, before retreating back into Sarah's room.

Until sunset spread its fulsome rays over the house, the Ghost Mother sat on Sarah's bed, wondering how to strengthen her fragile bond with Jack. Ah, ungrateful children! Ungrateful, complicated children! Why did they all have to be this way? Why was it always such a trial to gain their love?

But at least everything was out in the open now. No more pretending. Given time, he'd grow used to her and start to call her Mother, at first resentfully, then with more affection. She'd get him to love her, but not by force. She'd make him love her by being a beacon of love herself.

Plumping the pillows under her chin, she tried to relax, perhaps get some sleep. Sarah, of course, wouldn't let her. Isabella's death was all she wanted to talk about. Death. Death. There had to be a way to stop her doing that.

'So, how do you think Jack is taking to me?' she asked Sarah conversationally. 'He's a practical and intelligent boy. It can only be a matter of time before he comes to an acceptance of matters.'

'He'll never love you, if that's what you mean.'

'You think not? Better hope he does.' The Ghost Mother let her mind drift to the old swing in the garden; to knives in the kitchen, assorted sharp dangerous things; to accidental deaths, hints at murder.

'You wouldn't do that,' Sarah murmured.

'Wouldn't I? But didn't you yourself say I had already murdered my Isabella? If that is true, why should I not murder another child? And I have the means, now. I have your hands . . .'

'I can't believe –'

'That I'd hurt him? Are you sure? Perhaps I *should* kill him anyway. If Jack is dead, as long as I stop his loved ones taking him away, I'll have his soul all to myself, won't I? He'll have no way of getting away from me then. And he'll be a fresh soul, full of energy. It will be a long while before the Nightmare Passage comes to take him. I'll have all the time any mother could possibly need to wait for his love to flower. Of course, eventually, the Nightmare Passage will claim him. That will be a terrible moment, but I have lived through such moments before, and no doubt can again. Give me some peace or I will do it, Sarah. Don't force me to harm him. Don't make me harm our son.'

Sarah's voice fell quiet.

At last, the Ghost Mother thought, at last! A way to silence her!

Sighing, she stretched out her arms, wriggling against the sheets of the bed. She enjoyed their clean, soft feel. It was the first time she had been able to relax in her new body without Sarah's thoughts jabbing at her mind, and it was such a relief. Yawning, she massaged her stiff neck muscles. Then she realized that she felt tired – but not for sleep. All the battles with Sarah had worn her out.

Time for another meal.

The Ghost Mother walked across to the wardrobe. For a moment she stood there, idly scratching an itch on her wrist. Then she used the handsome brass key to unlock the wardrobe door.

She stared through the keyhole.

Oliver, of course, spat in her eye – a perfect aim.

Followed by a tirade of insults.

Still plenty of soul-energy left, the Ghost Mother thought. Good. She would need that to strengthen her over the next few days, until Jack came to accept her. After that it would be easier, though in the coming weeks and months there would obviously be further difficulties and trials. Fortunately, she had Charlie's and Gwyneth's souls in reserve. They were hiding somewhere, but they could not stay hidden forever. With the chill of the Nightmare

Passage passing like a warning across her fingers, the Ghost Mother reached into the depths of the wardrobe. She fought off Oliver's arms, and his well-aimed kicks, and forced his mouth open wide.

Seventeen
The Nightmare Passage

At first Ann did not know where she was. The light was too dim to see anything. There was no way to tell sky from ground, if those terms had any meaning here in the Nightmare Passage. She was aware only of ice crackling under her bare feet, and the howl of a searing, relentless wind. The wind blew in a single direction and it was unbearable.

Pulling her cotton slip over her feet, Ann hugged her knees. It made no difference. The wind drove into her, making her scream. For as long as she could she resisted, covering herself up, petrified about where the wind would take her if she gave in to it. Then she could hold on no longer – and the wind took her.

As soon as she was in motion she toppled headlong.

'No!' she cried, throwing her arms out wide.

The impact on the icy ground nearly broke her hands.

In terror, she realized that she no longer had the light, disembodied presence her soul had possessed in the farmhouse. That soul could easily have swept through the Nightmare Passage's winds and bounced harmlessly off the ground. Here she was heavy. Here she was the weight of a real body again. Her skin felt the raw sting of the ice. When she breathed every intake of air froze her lungs.

A shudder passed through her. We can't die here, she realized. We can't die again. We are souls. We're already dead. But we can feel everything. The Nightmare Passage gives us a flesh-and-blood body back, and the rules of pain are the same as for those with living bodies.

'Help me!' she shrieked.

Her voice swept up and away into the murk.

Was this the future for her now? A lost soul endlessly screaming from the darkness?

Then there was a rumble of thunder, and a brilliant flash – lightning – registered above her. It lasted only a fraction of a second, but that was all it took to see the Nightmare Passage for what it was.

It was nothingness. There were no objects to hide behind. There were no mountains or hills. There were no places that were better or worse. There was only a great, empty, featureless plain. The plain stretched on and on, endlessly in all directions. Even if she gave in to the wind, let it carry her for days, Ann sensed she would be no nearer or further from the Nightmare Passage's end, because there was no end. There was no point at which all the dead souls finally came crashing together, and were annihilated. There was just the journey across the plain, a journey whose only purpose was to cause pain.

The Nightmare Passage *was* the journey.

It was the wind and the plain and the journey across it, and it went on forever.

The sky – if it was a sky – soared miles above her head. In that brief flash of lighting she'd seen clouds, but they were so immense that they hardly seemed like clouds at all. Ann heard a further rumble of thunder, and the wind picked up, whipping around her. She couldn't believe it could get any colder, but it did, and she screamed again because that at least gave a little relief from the pain.

A third rumble, and through watering eyes Ann began to adjust to the feeble light illuminating the Nightmare Passage.

That's when she saw the first of the other lost souls.

It was a woman – wasn't it?

Ann couldn't be sure. Only a scrag end of colourless hair suggested it. Her face and body were too badly damaged for Ann to tell what age she might be. Apart from undergarments she was naked, except for a black legging hanging off one foot. Any other clothes she'd entered the Nightmare Passage with had obviously been ripped from her body by the rub of the ground. She didn't even move like a human being. She rolled across the plain towards Ann like a piece of discarded rubbish, making no effort to protect herself. As she toppled forward, one of her kneecaps struck the hard ground, then a shoulder-blade, then a soft part of her face.

Ann screamed, but the woman did not.

Next the woman's left forearm got caught awkwardly under her chest. For a moment, Ann saw it bend. Then the forearm snapped. Even over the wind, the break was audible. Ann screamed again, but the woman did not. Her eyes, however, opened when the bone cracked, and Ann noticed life of a kind there, a slow blink.

Seeing that, Ann tried to reach her, but the woman did not plead or reach out in any way for assistance. Tumbling beyond Ann's grasp, her lids just slowly opened and closed, blank eyes full of unimaginable hurt. Otherwise the woman made no sound at all, not even to cry out – as if all expectation of any kind of help had gone. She simply fell away into the distance, her eyes on Ann the whole time until her body, still toppling, being injured over and over again, receded against the grey horizon.

Ann became aware of movement around her.

There were other people in the Nightmare Passage. Once her sight adjusted to the murky light, she could see more of their broken, neglected bodies – including children – blowing like litter across the great plain. And, watching them, Ann at last began to understand something of the brutal reasons why this place was called the Nightmare Passage. Death itself would have been preferable to such suffering. Death would have been a relief. The residents of the Nightmare Passage longed for death. Instead, in a thousand ways, they were perpetually injured.

That was the horror of the Nightmare Passage.

To her left, six other people were dimly visible through the murk. From different locations they were heading towards her.

'Help me!' Ann shouted at them, waving her arms.

The six figures ignored her. Scrambling in a crab-like

way, staying low to the ground, they cut a path sideways through the wind. One – a girl about six years old – looking as wild as any animal, grinned at Ann and rolled her eyes until the whites showed. All of the figures were covered from head to foot in thick clothing. It was especially bunched around their joints and vulnerable areas. They continued to take no notice of Ann, heading doggedly for an object on the ice. It was the black legging, fallen from the woman's foot. Of course, Ann thought. Clothing must be the most valuable commodity in the Nightmare Passage, always shredding off on the ground. There would never be enough to cosset you from the cold.

'Who are you?' Ann screamed at them.

They did not answer, just relentlessly closed the gap between themselves and the legging, making odd threatening noises at each other, obviously prepared to fight over it if they had to. There was another flash of lighting, and this time Ann saw something massing behind her. It was a vast wall of wind, like a storm-wave crashing towards a beach. The wave was so immense and terrifying that Ann screamed – until she saw a child on its crest.

A boy was up there, riding the wave. He seemed to be almost dancing on the crest, making intricate movements of his feet as he strode laterally across it, heading towards her at a tremendous pace.

In front of her, the six figures studied the wave anxiously, then formed a ragged little line at its base. Just before it struck they jumped – and the wave picked them up and threw them onto its crest.

The sky was filled with thunder and lightning, but no rain. The boy, his arms held wide in the wind, soared closer. He leaped over the wild little girl, still tacking laterally across the wave top hundreds of feet above her, glanced at Ann and lifted his arms. He kept doing that, as if he wanted Ann to – what?

To jump.

Ann clenched her teeth and did. For a moment she sank into the wave, her jump poorly timed, the thick heavy air knocking away her breath. Then she lifted her face and knew she was free of it, high up in the sky.

The boy ran alongside her, clutching her hand, holding her up.

He grinned, and whooped. 'Hnya! Hnya!' he cried, or something like it – his voice so thin and dry Ann couldn't understand. He lifted her hands up in triumph. Ann saw sheer joy on his face. Either he was insane, or this wave was a good place to be in the Nightmare Passage, somewhere a child could be happy.

Other people were also on the wave top, riding it. She could see thousands of individuals now, mostly adults, but children as well, all moving with great deftness, dipping in and out of the crest like surfers, traversing the wave top.

The little wild girl slipped down the wave, holding the legging proudly in her hand, fighting off the others with her nails.

It wasn't as cold as it had been. In fact, it wasn't cold at all at this altitude in the Nightmare Passage. That's why the boy's whooping, Ann thought. Like all these other lost souls, he's staying warm. Warmth means happiness here.

A hat swaddled the boy's head, firmly tied on with a knotted scarf. Dozens of other layered bits of clothing covered the rest of his body. This is what I'll look like if I stay here long enough, Ann realized. If I'm lucky. If I can find enough clothes torn from people who've given up, like the woman.

Before she could ask the boy his name the wave collapsed. It happened fast, and Ann descended the crest, but the boy held her up, controlling her fall. She spilled with him safely out of the wave back to the icy ground.

There was no respite from the wind. It immediately picked her up again. Ann despairingly dug her heels in.

'Hnn?' the boy said.

He looked at her with feral blue eyes, and took off his hat.

Ann realized he was offering it to her for protection – an act of kindness.

She accepted it, letting him tie it on. The boy smiled. Then, with another whoop, he tumbled straight into the darkness.

Ann, frightened, tumbled after him, but her arms and knees kept jarring against the ice. 'I can't!' she said, stopping again. 'It hurts too much!'

The boy leaped in the air, dumbfounded that she'd spoken. Clearly no one had spoken to him for a long time. He gave a dry laugh, and touched her legs.

'What are you doing?'

He pointed to her, then himself.

'Copy you? Is that what you mean?'

'Rghn ma.'

The boy rolled himself into what to Ann looked like a foetally tight ball.

'Trust me?' Ann said.

The boy nodded, and whooped again, immensely

pleased that she understood. His teeth were the whitest Ann had ever seen. Polished by the wind, she realized. He had no real nails on his hands; at some point they had all been ripped off, and only partially grown back. There was an ugly scab on his nose where it had bled, re-healed, bled again, countless times, leaving a hard bony rind.

How long had he been in the Nightmare Passage? A month? A hundred years? Longer?

Ann got her body into a crouch like the boy's, and pulled in her legs. Instantly the wind swept her up, and she tumbled much faster than before. The tight position was hard to maintain – her muscles weren't used to it yet – but her body also travelled far more smoothly over the ground, and the wind bothered her less. The friction of her fast-rolling body also generated heat. She was warming up. The boy had taught her the only way to avoid freezing on the surface of the Nightmare Passage.

The wind abruptly ceased again, and she fell crazily out of her tumble to a halt. All around her the inhabitants of the Nightmare Passage immediately began checking them-selves, looking for injuries. The boy did the same, then examined Ann. Finding a bruise on her left calf, he tore a wedge of padding from an inner pocket and tied it carefully around the area. He smiled at her again, jauntily indicating the special padding around his neck, elbows and knees. He's proud of them, Ann realized. The clothing's not for warmth. There's no real warmth here. It's more like armour. Keeping their clothing intact, more than anything else, shows how well people are surviving here. Even in the Nightmare Passage, there was pride of a kind.

The boy smiled, showing Ann how to make the best of

her slip, using strange knots and wrapping it in tight layers around her knees and elbows. He obviously found its thin threadbare quality hilarious, though he also admired its softness. He kept sniffing it. Ann wondered why. Did her clothing still have a hint of the real world attached to it?

Then, without further ado, the boy tucked an arm under his head and fell asleep. Ann gazed around. All across the Nightmare Passage people were doing the same thing. Why? Was this the only chance to nap – the brief intervals between storm-waves?

The boy woke a few minutes later, when the wind picked up again.

'My name is –' Ann tried to speak, but her mouth was dry from the wind. She swallowed several times to line her throat with moisture. The boy tied part of his knee pad to her shoulder, and waited patiently. 'I'd have been hurt more,' she said at last, 'if you hadn't helped. If you hadn't shown me things. Thank you.'

He stared down curiously at the spot where she touched his arm, and as he turned away Ann realized with a jolt that something about the boy was familiar. Although she'd been with him all this time, it was only when he bent his head a certain way that she recognized an old gesture.

'Oh no,' she whispered.

She knew exactly how long this boy had been in the Nightmare Passage.

Forty-two years.

His face was utterly changed, weathered, scabbed, a horror story of pain and endurance, but it was still him. It was Daniel. She was sure of it. Ann put her hand to her mouth, looking down to compose herself.

'Ann,' she said, reaching out to him. 'It's . . . Ann. Don't you recognize me?' The boy continued to smile at her. 'I was with you in the farmhouse with the Ghost Mother. Ann. You don't remember, do you?'

Daniel, puzzled, examined her more thoughtfully. He felt her arms, especially the white cotton sleeves. He looked for a moment as if he didn't want to remember, that it was too painful, and turned away from her to look out over the vast empty reaches of the Nightmare Passage.

'I'm sorry,' Ann said, kissing him. 'You shouldn't have been here so long. It's my fault. I told you to disobey the Ghost Mother. I encouraged you. I shouldn't have. It made her angry. I didn't understand what would happen. Oh, look at you . . .'

'Thathiel,' he said quietly. He turned slowly back to her. 'Dathiel?' He seemed pleased to be saying his name again. It took him several attempts to pronounce it anywhere near clearly, and even then he couldn't quite get it right. There were portions of his throat, Ann realized, the endless cold had totally destroyed over the years.

The wind picked up again. There was no warning, no gradual transition from calmness to storm-force. All around them people glanced over their shoulders, judging what was to come next and how to prepare for it.

Daniel stared at Ann, saying something. At first Ann thought he was trying to say her name, but it wasn't that.

'A fforth nnnn,' he said, smiling. He patted her hand.

Another wave appeared on the horizon behind Ann. This one was twice the size of the last, and even the veterans of the Nightmare Passage looked anxious. There were urgent commands as people got into position.

'What do we do?' Ann asked. 'Ride it like the last one?'

Daniel smiled and cupped her face in his hands.

'I for than yeee,' he said. Ann had no idea what he was trying to tell her.

The wave closed in, a massive black shadow, and across the Nightmare Passage people stood up, leaning against the wind, preparing for it. But Daniel just kept smiling and stroking Ann's face, as if he'd not seen it at all.

'I ferths yee,' he said, stroking her face. 'I ferths yo.'

The dark wave consumed the overhead sky now. Ann could barely even see Daniel's face. He continued to stroke her and smile.

'We haven't got time for this,' she shouted, knocking his hand away. 'Look!' She pointed at the wave crashing towards them. 'We have to do something to get away from it! Show me what to do!'

Tears appeared on Daniel's face. He touched them with his fingers, then dabbed the wetness against Ann's dry lips.

'Stop it!' Ann wailed. 'Please, Daniel . . .'

He saw she did not understand. Smiling sadly, he grasped her hand and placed himself side-on to the massive oncoming wave, ready to jump.

'I forgith ou,' he whispered.

Eighteen

Bruised

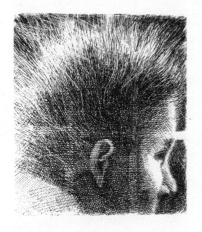

Oliver lay in the corner of Sarah's wardrobe, burning with anger. To have been captured so easily! The shame of it! The only good news, he thought, was that at least Charlie hadn't seen his pathetic struggle to hold the Ghost Mother off.

A weak crack of moonlight pierced the keyhole, but he couldn't escape that way. The Ghost Mother had taken too much of his soul to squeeze out. His mouth felt bruised from her grip, his cheeks like two aching hollows where she'd clamped her mouth over them. Oliver rubbed his jaw, smiling grimly to himself. She'd certainly enjoyed herself well enough. Her first feed had been a fast, greedy one; the second a deeper savouring that left him almost nothing.

Payback time.

He knew she'd come for him again. Maybe in the next hour, maybe later, but soon. One slim hope sustained him while he waited – that somehow he could *take her with him* into the Nightmare Passage. He'd been feeling its soft, almost playful, tugs at his hair for hours now, as it prepared to welcome him into its cold depths. Could he force the Ghost Mother to join him inside it? Maybe. If he could get close enough to her. If, when the Nightmare Passage came to claim his soul, she was feeding from him.

But to have any chance, Oliver knew he had to hold on until the Ghost Mother returned. She'd already fed from him twice. Come on, he thought. One more meal. It's me, Oliver! You can't have seen me suffer enough yet. Surely you're still hungry for more of that . . .

He stayed entirely still. The Nightmare Passage rustled with anticipation, tiny gusts flickering his face, but he disregarded them. Motionless, facing the wardrobe door, he waited for the Ghost Mother to come for him.

Nineteen

Snow

'You're back!' Jack whispered.

Isabella arrived in his bedroom that night more suddenly than the first occasion, ripped through from the Other Side. She screamed – it clearly caused her pain now – and floated precariously beside Jack's bed. He'd had no rocking chair this time to summon her, but he didn't need it. He already knew from before how to trace her; his gift, delving in so much death, was stronger than ever.

'I had no choice,' he apologized. 'I had to do it.'

She nodded. 'I cannot stay, Jack. It hurts too much. I want to help you, but I am not meant to be here any longer. I never was.'

The shadow branch of the garden tree shook against Isabella's face. It was her shaking, not the tree.

'Help me,' Jack pleaded. 'Your mother is inside mine. I don't know how, but she's taken her body. She wants me to love her. She wants kisses. I'll give her them if I have to, if it gets her out of Mum. Tell me what I need to do!'

Isabella raked her hair behind her ears, striding across to the window.

'If it is true . . . for her to steal like this, a living body . . . is extremely rare. Only the greatest need could allow it to occur. Oh, Mother, what horror have you become?'

Jack stood up angrily. 'Why didn't she just go to the Other Side, like you and everyone else? I know something terrible happened between you and your mother in this house. What was it? What aren't you telling me, Isabella?'

'On this matter I will keep my silence, Jack.'

'You didn't die normally. It wasn't just the illness, was it?'

'Do not press me on this, I beg you.'

'I have to. Forgive me.'

Jack walked towards Isabella, until part of her insubstantial body intersected with his. That hurt her again, but when she tried to pull away he wouldn't let her.

'I'm sorry, Isabella.'

There was an iron bed. On that bed Isabella, close to death, lay in her own sweat, daring herself to get up.

Now or never, she thought. Now or never.

She rose from the bed with enormous difficulty, needing to use the wall to steady her arm. Nearly swooning as she stood, she coughed and concentrated on opening her bedroom door. One day, she knew, perhaps tomorrow, perhaps the next day, she would no longer have the strength to open it on her own, but that time had not quite arrived yet.

It's all right, she thought. No one will know.

She shuffled in tiny hesitant steps along the landing, pausing often to rest. Her mother was out for the morning, on some errand, and when she reached her room, Isabella entered it like a thief. She had already thoroughly washed herself all over from the pitcher, so that she would not leave a mark of any kind.

The dress was draped across the back of a chair, ready for collection tomorrow. It was an unusual one, different hues of blue, heavily embellished. Not much seamstress work came her mother's way, but she was cheap and capable and had been asked to do some complicated embroidery at the waist and on the sash by one of the few local families that could afford such luxuries. It was not a remarkable dress by some standards, but in all her life Isabella had never been close to anything like it.

Walking over to the dress, she caught a glimpse of herself in her mother's bedroom mirror. She hated to see herself now, especially her face, the sunken eyes, the brown skin, the brown gums.

I'll do it, she thought. No one will know. Just this one time. I'll be careful.

Isabella Kate Rosewood put on the blue dress on the morning of January twenty-seventh in her mother's room. First she took off her cotton wrap and nightgown and discarded them like an old skin. Then, shivering, and standing there for a moment, scared to touch the dress at all, she memorized the exact way it hung over the chair.

The dress was full-length on her. The skirt, of course, was loose, and so was the waist as she stepped into it, but the material was rich and wonderfully unfamiliar against her skin. She wriggled into it, careful not to snag or damage any part, adjusted the neckline, and went over to see how she fetched in the mirror. She gave a small gasp as she regarded herself. Not so bad, she thought. With the right pose, and some padding, she could pass by in the street as something more than a skeleton. She wished she had decent footwear to try with it. Well, no matter. She put on her old hob-nailed boots – too wide for her thin feet now – and twirled slowly in the dress. Wearing it was wonderful. In fact, it gave Isabella such a surge of giddy happiness that she decided to take a greater risk.

She tottered down the staircase.

She had not been out in the garden since the early part of winter, and then always accompanied. Her mother barely allowed her out in winter at all, because the cold air always set off a coughing fit. But Mother was always over-protective. How, Isabella thought, could a little saunter down the garden be dangerous? She would be careful to cover her mouth, to protect her throat. Snow was in the air, but only a few flakes, nothing that would damage the dress. Isabella stared out at the whiteness longingly. She hadn't touched snow for more than a year. Her cough would start up in the wind, but what of that? It would start up anyway. She only had to be careful, surely, not to fall over, and she could take small steps to ensure that.

A small saucepan of vegetable broth had been left on the range by her mother. She forced it down, though she wasn't hungry; she rarely felt hungry these days. Sam followed her everywhere, as always, wagging his tail, hoping for the leftovers. She let him lick the bowl.

'Shall we go out?' Isabella asked him. 'Shall we go out and see the world again?'

Sam had no objection.

Isabella leaned against the glass of the kitchen window. There was nothing left of her except a remnant of body under a blue dress, but she had no thought for that. She laughed to herself and rubbed Sam's hairy old belly as she draped her shawl over her shoulders. Donning her outdoor bonnet, she opened the front door a crack and peered out. Not too cold. A breeze lifted the hem of the dress and Sam wagged his tail.

'Just for a minute, that's all,' Isabella said to herself, stepping out. 'Just to the top of the garden.'

She shuffled determinedly up the garden path with Sam alongside. By the time she reached the gate she was more tired than she expected to be, though at least she was not coughing. She rested, a steadying hand on the gate, enjoying the slightly ticklish feel of the dress. Then she headed back to the house, watching her step the whole way. Snowflakes drifted into her mouth. She grinned and held out her hands to catch more of them. Her feet were cold but she didn't care. Very carefully, bunching the dress material underneath her, making sure her shawl completely covered it, she eased herself down on the small lawn and looked up at the swirling white sky.

It was only when Isabella tried to get up that she realized there was a problem. The strength, the leverage she needed from her back, was not there. After so much time propped up in bed, and always having a helping hand from her mother, the wasted muscles would no longer lift her.

She tried again, managing to tip herself onto her side. For several minutes she attempted to push herself into a sitting position, but could not. Every part of her was getting cold now. For a while she kept her face off the ground. Soon she did not have strength even for that. 'Sam!' she cried out, and he trotted up to her, digging his nose curiously into her side, snuffling and wagging. 'Go fetch help! Go!' she told him, flinging out her arm to indicate the path.

Sam ran part-way up, then back. He didn't understand.

'Go on!' she encouraged him. 'Go on!'

The snow began to settle against the side of her face. After a few minutes she lost the strength to call out.

Isabella woke to find herself back in the house, her wet shawl removed. Her mother was bathing her in warm water by the hearth. The blue dress, thrown across a chair, was sodden and ruined.

'I'm sorry!' Isabella wept. 'What have I done? The cost of –'

'Shush now, it doesn't matter,' her mother replied softly. She washed Isabella's shivering legs.

'Can it . . . be repaired?' Isabella asked.

'Of course I can repair it. It will not take much effort at all.'

'Oh, why did I go out? I only –'

It was then that the cough erupted. It wasn't the familiar cough this time. It was thicker, heavier. Isabella tried to focus on her mother, but could not. She felt only an intense nausea. 'I have to sit up.' She could feel the contents of her stomach loosening, and rose up enough to be sick, and it was red, red. It was not the food from earlier. It was red, all over the blanket, the floor, her mother, who held her, and still it came forth.

Isabella, in Jack's bedroom, stared at him fiercely.

'I didn't die,' she said. 'Not then. But I wish I had. Go on!' she challenged him. 'You wanted to see! You forced me back here! You wanted to know everything! What's stopping you! Not I!'

'Isabella . . .' Jack let go of her, but she reached for him again.

'No,' she said, pressing her body up to his. 'All of it. All of it!'

Three weeks had passed. In all that time not once had Isabella been well enough to leave the upper house. The fire in her room was lit every day, however, by her mother. Only that kept her clinging onto life.

Apart from Isabella and Sam, the house was empty. Her mother was out again. Isabella did not know where. She rarely said what she was doing these days. It took Isabella over half an hour to make her way down the stairs. When she stumbled into the kitchen she felt her way along the walls until she reached the chair, and sat down in it.

The kitchen was bitterly cold. The rest of the house was bitterly cold. Only her room was being heated, she realized. The ruined blue dress was in a corner of the room. Isabella saw where her mother had tried to repair the dress, but it was not possible. The cost of replacing it was beyond belief. Isabella could only imagine how much extra work her mother was having to take in to do so. There were men's working boots on the floor, in need of repair. Isabella did not know her mother had started taking in boots. There was also a list of the houses she was to clean today in her mother's clear handwriting near the fireplace. She had skilfully concealed from Isabella how she had become a skivvy for half the houses in the village.

Isabella glanced at the range, and saw two saucepans. One held the remains of a potato stew her mother had fed her before she left. The second was a watery soup made from boiled meat bones. They were horse bones.

This was her mother's food.

Isabella wept, and looked at Sam. He sat, thin as a whippet, by her feet.

'I was not meant to see any of this,' Isabella whispered to him. 'Sam, you should have told me. She'll die before me, won't she?' She rubbed his muzzle. 'No. We can't have that. We can't allow that. We can't.'

It was a freezing day outside. Heavy snow gusted and drifted against the side of the house. Isabella stared out at it. She narrowed her eyes, then smiled at Sam.

'Will you accompany me one more time into the garden?'

Without putting on her boots, she opened the front door. An icy wind cut in at once, and she thought the door would blow back and knock her down, but she held it until the gust was gone. Her bonnet was by the door. She left it there.

Her cough started up as soon as the cold penetrated the swollen damaged passages of her throat. Isabella ignored it. Barely able to make it out through the thick snow underfoot, she shuffled over to the flowers she could reach. They were mostly hidden under the snow, and there were more weeds than she expected. Her mother had not had the energy to keep up the garden this year.

Next year, perhaps.

For a moment, as Isabella bent towards a rose thorn, the sun came out. It was low on the horizon, and not warm, but Isabella blinked at it through the snow and smiled. A robin saw her and flew off. Sam chased it for a few seconds, then sniffed Isabella's feet.

'Come here,' Isabella said.

She lay down on the snow with him, and kissed his head.

Sam stayed next to her. After a while, restless, he slipped away. He ran towards the gate and back. He kept doing that. He knew something was wrong, but what? Isabella stayed still. She did not shout for help. The snow began to cover her mouth. Gradually the cold bothered her less, then not at all. Sam trotted back and forward from the gate, increasingly concerned, whimpering, nuzzling her face. After an hour he started to howl.

Isabella gave Jack one more memory. The second she died he saw her soul rise up from the snowy garden. He expected it to be her death-face, the one pinched against the cold, he saw, but Isabella had already left that behind. The face Jack saw was full of new life, and as it hesitantly looked up, the sky opened and the loved ones came for her, and the first of them to reach her was her father. Smiling, she held out her skinny arms to him and he took hold of them, and cradled her face, and carried her away into the whiteness of the clouds.

In the bedroom, Jack and Isabella sat together on the floor. For a long time they watched the moon and a sprinkling of stars on the eastern horizon, saying nothing. Then Isabella looked at Jack. 'Did you really think my mother would kill me?' she whispered. 'Did you really think she could ever have done that?'

Jack stared down, breathing heavily.

Isabella's face was bathed in moonlight.

'I must go now,' she said, clearly in enormous pain. 'The Other Side is calling me. If I stay any longer, the Nightmare Passage will claim me. Don't let that happen, Jack. Let me go.' She touched his face. Her hand passed through him, and she smiled regretfully. 'Remember me, Jack,' she whispered. 'When you die, an old man many years from now, and perhaps far from here, I will be waiting for you.'

'Isabella, not yet . . . don't . . .'

Jack reached out to her, but she was already fading.

'Dream of me,' she murmured. 'Dream of me, and I'll dream of you. Try to remember me.' She managed to say one more thing before she departed. 'The longer my mother is inside yours, the more damage she may do to her. If all else fails, remind her of her name. It is Mary Eloise. She responded to that name dearly enough once. If all else fails, remind her of who she once was . . .'

'Isabella!' Jack called out. 'Wait! Before you go, what is life on the Other Side like? My dad's there. I have to know!'

Her voice came in a whisper towards him.

'It is a better place, Jack. A . . .' He could barely hear her last words. '. . . kinder place. Goodbye, Jack. Close your eyes.'

'No. Let me see you leave. I . . . I want to see the Other Side. I need to.'

She set her lips, fixing her gaze on Jack – as if daring him to watch. And then her body blurred into a windless grey gale, mist and dress, and for a moment Jack glimpsed something utterly warm and pure behind.

Then she was gone. Jack listened, thinking that if he stayed quiet and concentrated he might still be able to hear her voice. But he could not. The room was entirely dark and silent. The only indication that Isabella had ever been within it was a faint sway of the curtains.

He sat down on the bed and stared at the wall.

'Isabella Kate Rosewood,' he whispered. 'I will. Of course I'll remember you.'

Twenty

The Knife

For a few minutes Jack sat back, remembering what Isabella's fading body had looked like in the moonlight, and wondering about the damage being done to his mum. Then he heard the softest of footfalls outside his bedroom door.

'Jack, are you awake?'

He barely had time to lie down before the door swung open. There was no chance to pull the duvet over his legs. The door creaked as the Ghost Mother swept into the room. Standing over his bed, she gazed down at him.

In her hand there was a knife.

The knife was six inches long. It was one of the biggest of the kitchen cutting knives, with a pine-wood handle indented for easy gripping. The Ghost Mother held it casually, the tip pointed towards the ceiling. Part of Jack knew there must be an innocent explanation for its presence in her hand, but he couldn't take his gaze off it.

His airway constricted — the shock initiating an asthma attack.

'I thought I heard your voice,' the Ghost Mother said.

She saw him staring at the knife, and her eyes widened in understanding.

'I am your mother!' she shrieked. 'Do you think I would use a knife against my own flesh and blood? I couldn't sleep,' she explained. 'I was preparing food for tomorrow. I . . . Jack?'

Jack tried to speak, but his throat was too tight. He knew his only chance to stop the attack was to get to his medication quickly. Staggering upright, he reached for the inhaler on his bedside table, took a full dosage and waited. There was no improvement. He needed the extra chemicals in his beta-agonist supplemental inhaler.

'My medicine . . .'

'I will take care of you, Jack.'

'You . . . you don't understand. My medicine. I . . . need to get . . .'

He stumbled past her to the bathroom, couldn't find the emergency inhaler, then found it, sat on the toilet seat and sucked out four dosages. It took Jack over twenty minutes to get his breathing back to a regular rhythm. The Ghost Mother tried laying a hand on his back to hearten him, but he swatted it away and, though it upset her, she did not touch him again. She allowed him to close the bathroom door for privacy, though she remained outside. He could hear her anxious pacing.

I can't do this, he thought. I can't talk to her about Isabella. Not now.

He slumped to his knees on the bathroom floor. He

wanted nothing more than to stay there, curled up next to the toilet until morning, and wake to find his real mother calling him down to breakfast. Mum's being hurt, he thought. Damaged. I've got to find a way to get the Ghost Mother out of her!

'Jack?' The Ghost Mother's voice.

'I'm . . . OK.'

'Can I see you?'

'I'll . . . be out soon. I just need a minute . . . a few minutes . . .'

She cleared her throat to reply, then changed her mind.

When he left the bathroom he found her reclining in one of the lounge armchairs, waiting for him. The knife was gone. She'd also changed into Sarah's chocolate-brown dressing gown. For some reason that infuriated him.

'Are you better, Jack? Are you well?'

He didn't bother answering.

She lowered her eyes, then raised them again.

'I have been thinking,' she said. 'I want you to have things. Your mother bought you presents. I could buy you presents as well. Is that what you'd like?'

'No.'

She smiled, his answer pleasing her.

'I did not think so. One cannot judge how much one is loved by gifts, can one, Jack? One judges it in other ways. By what one says. By what one does. I will always be here for you.'

Jack said nothing.

'Come to me,' she murmured.

'Why?'

Irritation creased her face. 'Why do you always give such brief or snappish replies? Indulge me, Jack. Come here.'

'I have . . . something to say to you. I know what happened to –'

'Shush.' She put a finger to her lips. 'I am sure you have much to say to me, and I wish to hear it. But first, come here.'

Jack remained where he was.

'Stay away from me!' he shouted. 'I mean it!'

'The knife . . . if it was the knife . . .'

'It's more than the knife. It's *you*! You're not my mother! Stop pretending to be my mother! Stop –'

The constriction in his chest returned. This time it nearly bent him over backwards.

The Ghost Mother sidled up to him.

'Calm yourself, Jack.'

'Get . . . away . . . from me!'

While he still had some control of his breathing, Jack struck out at her, but his fists in that moment had no strength. Blocking his hands, her arms gathered him up. He struggled against her, but she hugged him, and finally Jack realized that the only way he could survive was to let her. So he stayed in her embrace, his flesh crawling at her touch, until his breathing came back to something like normal.

After many silent minutes, the Ghost Mother broke the embrace.

'You see,' she whispered, 'you don't need your old mother after all. She never took care of you the way I will.' She smiled. She had never looked more relaxed and comfortable. 'I want to show you something, Jack.' She took his hand firmly.

Jack yanked it away, but the Ghost Mother cornered him and reached out again.

'Get away from me!' he rasped, unable to stop her.

'Let me do away with all these fears once and for all,' she murmured, taking his hand. 'I have something to show you, Jack.'

'I don't want any more of your memories!'

'One more. Nothing will be the same after it.'

It was late afternoon before Mary Eloise Rosewood found her daughter lying in the snow-blown garden. Her return had been delayed partly by the atrocious weather and partly by a client who questioned her workmanship on a perfectly-scrubbed floor, forcing her to do it again.

By the time she returned Isabella, of course, was dead.

With Sam running in anxious circles around her, Mary Eloise lifted Isabella with both arms – an easy weight – and took her into the house. She carried her up the stairs to Isabella's room, and wiped the snow out of her eyes. Undressing her, she wrapped Isabella in every warm thing in the house, talking to her as if she was still alive.

And then she began to scream.

Later, she arranged Isabella's body out on the bed sheets, placing cold flowers from the garden around her head. She stayed there until sunset, then went out into the garden. She looked for signs of a struggle, that Isabella had accidentally got herself in trouble like last time, but of course there were no such signs. Isabella's footprints led in a straight line from the house to this spot in the garden.

Her shoes were still in the house, and her bonnet. She'd obviously wanted to rush away from this world before anyone could stop her.

Mary Eloise walked back to the kitchen. She saw the ruined blue dress she'd lied about, the list of houses to clean, the men's boots. She saw the horse bones congealed in the pan – all left in plain sight for Isabella to see. She'd been in such a rush this morning, and Isabella had not been up in weeks. And then she had come down and seen . . .

Mary Eloise returned to Isabella's room and unlatched the window. She pushed it wide, wedging it open. Then she removed all her clothing, and instead put on only a thin black mourning dress that would be no protection against the cold. She tore that dress at the collar, and crammed herself into Isabella's wooden rocking chair. It was still freezing outside, snowflakes drifting through the window.

Mary Eloise Rosewood sat there, willing herself to die. It took longer than she expected. Although she starved herself, and did not drink, and she was already half-dead anyway from malnutrition, her body was not as willing as her mind. It clung onto life, refusing to die. It was three days before her heart finally gave up.

And then, the moment her final breath was gone, they came, of course – her loved ones flying from the skies. They arrived with eagerness, and they tried to draw her out gently with them, but she would not go. They begged her, but she refused. What right had she to be drawn gently anywhere after causing Isabella's suicide? Denying herself even a glimpse of Isabella, racked with guilt, her soul drifted away from them all. Her dress was black and her mind was black, and she floated like a dense black patch through the wintry rooms, screaming at them to go. Fighting off the pleading arms clutching at her, she sank into the depths of the house until she reached the cellar. There she waited for the loved ones to leave. A single presence stayed with her for the longest time. Mary Eloise turned aside, weeping, ignoring it.

Later, after the wind died down, she drifted back up to Isabella's room again. She sat there, atop her own dead body, and stared out of the window. She saw the fields, the horizon, the edge of the wood. It was still snowing slightly, but milder. She didn't want that. She wanted to be back in the chair, freezing to death. She hadn't been punished enough.

She gazed out, longing for the hurt of snow.

A neighbour of Mary Eloise found her stiffening body half-frozen to the arms of the rocking chair. To ensure she got a proper Christian burial on consecrated ground she prised her off the chair, closed the window, carried her body to the top of the stairs and let her fall, as if it had been an accident. To anyone investigating the death of the mother and daughter the circumstances would have been suspic-ious, but they were poor and no one investigated. An elderly relative neither Isabella nor Mary Eloise ever liked took all their possessions and sold them for what he could get. The wooden rocking chair was overused and worth little, so he dragged it to the cellar and left it there. Business affairs kept him from staying for the burial.

The funeral was attended by two pallbearers and the local priest. Mary Eloise's spirit watched from the house, denying herself even the right to attend. The pallbearers lowered two coffins into the ground. One was small. Five feet by two was enough for Isabella. The mother's was larger, but they were not placed side by side, because there was not enough room. The pallbearers were the only witnesses to hear the local priest say prayers and see the bodies interred, except for an old white and brown terrier that wagged its tail uncertainly at so many strangers.

The Ghost Mother, in the lounge, slowly released her grip on Jack's hand.

'Well,' she said huskily, 'so there it is. Now you understand it all. Everything a poor wretched mother has to show.' She sighed. 'I did not deserve to leave with my loved ones, you see that, don't you, Jack? Not until I'd been punished further. How could I let Isabella whisper me away to the Other Side so soon, when but for my neglect she would have been with me still?' She smiled sadly. 'It cost one pound and ten shillings in my day to bury a child cheaply. At least I was spared the torment of gathering that sum together.'

Jack stared out of the window, his feelings still being stirred by everything she'd shown him.

'I see you are quite emotional about it all,' the Ghost Mother said. 'You should not be, Jack. After all your time in this house, by now you are quite used to seeing the dead, surely, and children of that time were also. It was nothing remarkable for a boy or girl to find their best friend too ill to play one morning, and dying the next. To most, Isabella was just another such child. Sam did not forget her, though. After the funeral he howled outside the house for three days before he left. I have no idea what happened to him. I hope he found a home.'

Jack stared thoughtfully at the Ghost Mother.

He knew the memories she'd shown him were true ones – but something was missing. There was nothing about the ghost children in what she'd revealed. Those memories clearly weren't ones she wanted him to see.

He faced her. 'You never told me your name,' he said. 'Not once. Not even when I asked you. When did you stop feeling you deserved a name, Mary Eloise Rosewood?'

The Ghost Mother caught her breath, and stepped back.

'You don't like being reminded of what you were before, do you? Why? How much has living in this house changed you?'

'Jack, go no further with this.'

She gave him a warning glance. Jack ignored it.

'The ghost children think you're a monster. What you've shown me isn't everything, is it? What are you hiding from me, Mary Eloise? What happened to you after Isabella died?'

The Ghost Mother chewed her lip.

'Jack, please . . . can't we make a new start now? I'll be whatever kind of mother you want. If you don't want me to look like this –'

'I want my *real* mother back! Not you. My real mother! Why can't you understand that?'

'I *am* your real mother now.'

Jack stared at her, dumbfounded.

'You're not!'

'I am.' She stood still, smiling at him helplessly.

'You don't even look like her! You think you do, but you don't! Your face is all wrong.'

'I can change that. Give me time.'

'No, you'll never be her! Never! Tell me what did you do to the ghost children!'

She stared at him, suddenly furious, all patience gone.

'The ghost children! The ghost children! Will you *never* cease to thrust them at me?' She raked her fingers against her dressing gown. 'I do not want to hear mention of them again. Do I make myself plain?'

She marched him to his bedroom. Jack did not hide his look of hatred before she shut the door in his face. Then she went downstairs, and there was a brief jingling of keys. Was she going out? His hopes were raised until he heard her tramp back up. From outside his room she sorted through a bunch of keys until she found the one she wanted. Jack didn't even know his room could be locked until she inserted the key and turned it.

Twenty-one

The Wardrobe

'Anyone there? Oliver! Are you in there?'

A whisper outside the wardrobe. At first Oliver thought it must be the Ghost Mother, come in the night for her third meal. Then, through the crack in the keyhole, he saw a boy floating in the bedroom darkness.

'Charlie! What's going on? You shouldn't be anywhere near this place! She'll find you! Get back to Gwyneth!'

'I'm here, too,' Gwyneth's voice piped up.

'What?' Oliver hissed. 'Charlie, you idiot, what are you doing?'

'I had to bring her! She wouldn't stay there on her own.'

'Go now! Get out! Both of you!'

'I'm not leaving you here!' Charlie shouted back.

'You have to! There's nothing you can do for me. Just get out before –'

'Before what?' A more seductive voice.

Gwyneth cringed and Oliver looked through the keyhole to see the Ghost Mother standing at the threshold of the room, casually leaning against the door frame.

'All three of you together,' she said. 'I knew if I waited long enough you'd come, Charlie. Oliver's right. You should have stayed hidden.'

She walked rapidly across the room and opened the wardrobe. A shaft of moonlight briefly blinded Oliver, then he saw the Ghost Mother picking Charlie and Gwyneth up. For a moment she held them both close to her face, as if choosing which to feed upon.

'What about me?' Oliver shouted. 'Forgotten me, have you? You think I'm finished?'

The Ghost Mother ignored him. Gwyneth screamed as her head was bent forward and lifted. Then the Ghost Mother changed her mind, dropped Gwyneth and turned instead to Charlie. Gwyneth wafted aimlessly above the floor, petrified.

Oliver shouted, 'Gwyneth, get out! Get out now!'

Stung into action, she caught a backdraught out of the room and fled – but slowly. It was the best she could do.

The Ghost Mother followed her. Oliver concentrated, swearing and taunting her as richly as he could. Eventually, she reacted.

'You really want me to feed off you again?' she challenged him from the doorway. 'You know what will happen if I take any more of your soul? Is that what you truly want, Oliver?'

'Come on, if you dare!' Remembering what she'd done before, he crooked his finger invitingly.

The Ghost Mother hesitated, then pulled not Oliver's

but Charlie's face towards her. Making sure Oliver got a good view, she planted a full seal around Charlie's lips and took a long drink of his soul. Oliver swore and tried to float towards her, but he was now so weak that every tiny breeze in the room blew him wherever it wanted.

'Leave him alone! I've still got more to give than Charlie!'

'Very well.' The Ghost Mother took two steps towards the wardrobe, and plucked Oliver out of the air. She held both boys at head height. Charlie stared at her, panting with shock. He had been in the house much longer than Oliver, and his soul was already precariously close to the Nightmare Passage.

Oliver felt a shadow block out the moon, then an uncomfortable pressure as the Ghost Mother's lips pressed expertly against his.

Go on, he thought. Drink deep. Take it all.

But she only took a morsel this time before withdrawing. The Nightmare Passage clung to every part of him.

'I see what you are trying to do, Oliver. You'll not get me that way.'

She pushed him back inside the wardrobe, along with Charlie.

'Afraid to get close to me now?' Oliver said. 'Come on, one more sip!'

The Ghost Mother kept her distance, staring at him.

Oliver stared back. He felt the Nightmare Passage fully now, almost ready to claim him. There were already holes in the palms of both his hands. He reached out with them to the Ghost Mother, and she jerked back.

'Scared?' Oliver whispered. 'Come here!'

With the last of his strength he thrust himself forward.

An air current carried him towards the Ghost Mother – and she ran to the door. Following close behind, the coldness of the Nightmare Passage fully entered the room. It passed swiftly through the gaps of Oliver's hands, then wrapped itself around his left leg, smashing a hole in his thigh. The Ghost Mother screamed as something numb broke over her face.

'No,' she said. 'I won't let you take me as well!'

She backed out to the landing. A moment later she hurriedly pushed a bathroom towel up against the bottom of the door.

'Come back here!' Oliver shouted. Floating about the room, he felt free for a few seconds, cold but free. 'I'll take you with me! I will!'

The Nightmare Passage was ready to claim him, but Oliver resisted it. He ignored the moon shining through his chest, and his disappearing hands. With everything he had, he screamed and held the Nightmare Passage back.

On the landing, the Ghost Mother stood against one of the walls, shaking with fear. She stared at the bottom of Sarah's door, terrified that even with the towel in position Oliver would find a way out.

I'll . . . leave him there, she thought. Even Oliver can't fight off the Nightmare Passage for long. I won't go back in until I'm sure he's gone.

She trembled, collecting her thoughts. I need more energy, she decided. Jack won't love me yet. I need more energy to get through the difficult days ahead. I need

Gwyneth. Which way had she gone? Towards the lower house?

The Ghost Mother rushed down the stairs and searched the kitchen. No sign there. She checked the lounge, then backtracked to the scullery, in time to catch a glimpse of yellow nightie floating towards a crack between the floor and the wall. She ran towards it, clutching at the trailing ends of Gwyneth's hair, but with a shriek Gwyneth squeezed the last of herself into the crack.

Poking around in the kitchen cutlery drawer, the Ghost Mother picked out a steel skewer and tried to jab Gwyneth out, but by then she was deep down under the joists.

'I won't hurt you,' the Ghost Mother said gently. 'Come out. I only want to talk to you. Come on, let's talk, Gwyneth. I promise I won't do anything to you. You can hear me, can't you? Why won't you come out?' She listened, thought she heard whispering. 'Gwyneth? Please come out . . .'

A mouse, hidden until now, made a break for it, scrambling into the same gap Gwyneth entered. There was a squeal from inside, and this time the Ghost Mother could clearly hear Gwyneth feverishly whispering.

'Six, seven, eight –'

The mouse scuttled along the joist, and Gwyneth squealed again.

'Come back here,' the Ghost Mother said. 'I'll help you, Gwyneth. I'll protect you from it. Come out and be with me.'

Inside the crack, Gwyneth closed her eyes as something swift and hairy brushed past her. She continued to count.

Twenty-two

Only Darkness

———

Jack listened at his locked bedroom door, hearing terrible things going on. He had no idea what was happening, but he knew he had to get out of the house quickly. Isabella had said that the longer the Ghost Mother remained inside his mum, the more damage she did. Waiting, biding his time to sneak away, was probably the safest course of action, but what use was that to his mum? I'll let the Ghost Mother kiss me as often as she wants, he thought, but I have to get help fast for mum from somewhere.

How could he gain the Ghost Mother's trust? By being more obedient, of course. It was the only way. So stop yelling, he thought. Stop fighting her. Give her the respectful son she wants, until she relaxes and you can slip out.

About an hour later the Ghost Mother unlocked his door – but did not come in.

Jack waited a decent interval, practising queasy smiles in his mirror, then slowly made his way downstairs. He found the Ghost Mother in the lounge, sitting on a chair in the darkness. When she didn't respond to one of his fake new smiles he complimented her instead, and that worked better, because he didn't go too far with his praise. He said he enjoyed her plainer appearance and some, not all, of her new food. Knowing what she'd like best of all, he cleared away the ashes from the last fire and got a new one underway. Once the sticks were alight, he made himself sit on the sofa beside the Ghost Mother. He sat very close.

She gave him a tender look, and gazed into the fire.

Jack gazed tenderly back. To make her feel more comfortable he took her arm and wrapped it around his waist.

Her eyes misted over a little.

'I would like to hope,' she said, 'that the small difficulties between us will soon be matters of the past. I do not wish to play games forever, where we force ourselves into smiles and every manner of pretence.' She stared meaningfully at him.

'I'm not pretending,' Jack said, looking directly at her. 'I'm tired of fighting you, that's all.'

Enduring the sweltering fire, he stayed close by her until the early hours of the morning. He watched TV with her, chatted amiably. He made sure no silly new arguments flared up between them. Before he went to bed he even screwed up his nerve and made a point of giving the Ghost Mother a good-night kiss. It was a proper son-to-mother kiss, the best he could manage, and afterwards he made his way somewhat unsteadily to his room. Changing into his pyjamas, he murmured a final 'good night' down the hall, shut his door and collapsed on his bed, exhausted.

Once he'd calmed down, he carried out his peak flow number test. The asthma reading veered between amber and red – extreme danger. Looking at the gauge, Jack knew he wasn't going to be able to keep up the good-boy act after all. But she's probably just as likely to be watching me closely tomorrow or the next day, he thought. I should do it tonight, if I can. That's better for mum, anyway. Get out before morning.

At 02:48 a.m. the Ghost Mother put the guard up against the fire, came up the stairs and listened outside his door a moment. Then she went into Isabella's room. Jack heard the rocking chair gently creaking on the floorboards for about an hour, followed by silence. He waited another hour before getting dressed in the darkness. No outdoors wear to start with, nothing he couldn't explain if she caught him. He padded down to the kitchen, made a ham sandwich and sat at the dining table munching mechanically away, waiting to see if she appeared.

Outside it was already a little brighter than he expected. A fading crescent moon peeped out from a cloud, as if encouraging him, and dawn was waking the birds.

Was she asleep? Surely even she had to sleep some-times . . .

He returned to his bedroom, more quietly this time, slung his shoes in a carrier bag and tiptoed back downstairs. No way of explaining it away if she caught him now, of course.

The front door was locked, but the keys were in the door.

Would it be as simple as unlocking it and walking away?

Or was she testing him?

No way to tell.

Jack eased his shoes and coat on, before turning his attention to the lock. He winced at the noisy, complex sound as the old mechanism cranked open. Still no sound from the rest of the house, except the perpetual loud ticking of the grandfather clock.

He undid the double bolts of the door, using tiny jiggling motions.

Holding his breath, he put his hand on the catch.

The door opened surprisingly quietly.

He pushed it wide and looked out into the night.

Then – he couldn't help it – he glanced one more time over his shoulder.

And there she was.

The Ghost Mother stood at the end of the hall, fully dressed. Her arms were folded. The rising dawn cast a straight bar of light across her throat.

It *had* been a test, after all.

'I'm . . .'

Jack couldn't manage to form any words as she ran at him. She grasped the hand holding the keys savagely, and used his fingers to re-lock the door before throwing the keys into the hall. Then she hauled him to the stairs. Her face was set, furious. 'You promised . . . you lied . . . you lied! Now there will be new rules to follow in this household!' She dragged him up the staircase.

'Let me go!'

She threw him down on the floor of his bedroom. Jack

felt his asthma bubbling up, and breathed slowly to compensate.

'All right,' he said, thinking furiously. 'I'll . . . I'll do it. I'll do anything you want.'

She stared at him, surprised. 'What did you say?'

'You heard me. I said I'll do anything you want.'

'You will accept my rules?'

'Yes.'

The Ghost Mother gazed at him suspiciously, but Jack had got her attention and now he stood up. He had to do this standing up. Maybe he could *shock* the Ghost Mother out of his mum? That's what he was thinking. What would shock her the most? What would force her to listen?

'It was cold that morning Isabella went out, wasn't it?' he said. 'It was freezing that day. Snowing.'

The Ghost Mother's face drained of colour.

'How dare you mention her name! I have told you –' She hesitated, then slapped his face hard. 'That is the last time you will ever speak her name again! The very last!'

'Listen to me!'

But she would not. She shoved him onto his bed, and raised her arm again. Jack was so sure she was going to hit him a second time that he picked up the bedside lamp to defend himself.

'Things will be different!' she yelled. 'Do you hear me?' Her hands beat her chest. 'I have . . . tried and tried! What else must I do to prove myself? Am I to be under trial forever by my own son? Does any mother deserve such treatment?' Her lips were white with rage. 'Do not push me too far, Jack,' she warned. 'I mean it. I have my limits!

Do not take me beyond that which any mother can be expected to endure!'

He heard the sinister change in tone, and knew she expected an immediate apology. No, he thought. Damn her. I won't.

He jumped off his bed, and barged past her onto the landing.

'You've stopped going in here, haven't you?' he said, flinging open Sarah's bedroom door. 'Why? What's in here you're so scared of?'

The Ghost Mother shrank back from the open doorway, her hand against her mouth, expecting Oliver to come flying towards her with the Nightmare Passage clinging to his back. When he did not, she knew the Nightmare Passage had taken him. Breathing a heavy sigh of relief, she walked inside the room and looked around.

'The children are in here, aren't they?' Jack said.

'The children, the children,' the Ghost Mother muttered. 'Do you never stop talking about them!' Then she stopped, and slowly turned to him, a changed look on her face. Her expression was still angry, but there was a new silkiness to her tone.

'Perhaps you want to see what I do with them, Jack? What I do to the children? You are always asking questions about them, after all. Perhaps I should answer some of them.'

'Just let me see that they're all right,' Jack replied nervously.

'Very well.'

The Ghost Mother unlocked the wardrobe.

'Oliver has joined Ann in the Nightmare Passage,' she

said, smiling. 'As for the shining knight who came to his rescue . . .' She opened the wardrobe door and reached inside. Charlie was crammed in the back. He raised his arms to protect himself, but the Ghost Mother easily brushed his tenuous hands aside.

There was someone else in the wardrobe with Charlie. Earlier, the Ghost Mother had smashed her way methodically through the floorboards of the larder until she reached Gwyneth. Even cringing next to the mice had not saved her. Now, as the Ghost Mother picked Charlie up by the neck, Gwyneth clung onto him, swinging loosely from his legs.

'This is what I do to them,' the Ghost Mother said to Jack, plucking Gwyneth off. 'You have driven me to this. I hope you are satisfied.' She upended Charlie and thrust his face against her lips.

Jack yelled and ran at the Ghost Mother, but she knocked him aside with the outside of her arm. His skull struck the frame of the bed. The pain was blinding – and his asthma exploded.

No, he thought. Not now. Not now!

He started to hyperventilate, breathing twice as fast, knowing that was making it worse, but unable to stop himself.

The Ghost Mother stared indifferently down at him. Charlie did not have the strength to resist her. She held him in both hands, taking lengthy swallows from his face, pausing only to let Jack see what she was doing. Then she did the same to Gwyneth.

Jack's inhaler was back in his bedroom. The biggest attack of his life was coming.

The Ghost Mother withdrew her mouth from Gwyneth, went back to Charlie, and Jack heard a rustle from the corner of the room. He looked up to see Charlie's face disappearing into the Nightmare Passage. Gwyneth held on a little longer. Her legs flopped, then drifted upward on the air. Wiping her lips, the Ghost Mother stared at Jack. 'See what you have forced upon me!'

'Don't hurt her any more,' Jack managed to whisper. 'I'll . . . I'll do anything you want. I'll . . . be . . . anything you want.'

'You'll never love me.'

'Please . . . I will . . .'

'No. I am done with you now, Jack, done with you.'

The Ghost Mother rubbed her lips dry to improve the contact, then clamped herself to Gwyneth again. Jack couldn't do anything to stop her. He gasped, trying to get more air into his lungs. I'm going to black out, he realized. If I do, the Ghost Mother will be able to do whatever she wants. I can't . . . let her . . .

He shifted his weight, giving his lungs as much room as he could, but it was no use. A slick sweat ran down his neck. He began to shake.

Gwyneth floated helplessly in the air, discarded. She tried to raise her head, find a way out of the room, but could not. The Ghost Mother yanked her up again, grazing in a leisurely way at her lips – but this time stopped quickly. Even Jack, almost unconscious, felt the coldness invading the room.

The Nightmare Passage had come for the last of the ghost children.

It tore a hole in Gwyneth's neck, and she screamed.

The Ghost Mother retreated towards the door.

For a moment Gwyneth looked more astonished than terrified. She put a hand inside the gap of her neck to see what was there. Only darkness. Jack fell unconscious with Gwyneth's screams ringing in his ears.

Twenty-three
The Everlasting Twilight

Daniel's wind-whitened teeth gleamed.

Ann had heard his words of forgiveness over the wind, and as he carried her into the high, safer reaches of the upper wave, she looked into his eyes and felt like crying. They weren't a boy's eyes. They were appallingly lined and wrinkled. Squinting against the wind made them look old, she realized. I'll be like him soon.

Looking around her at the desolation of the Nightmare Passage, she felt herself shrivelling. Even the agonized soul of the Ghost Mother, and the others like her who had refused for one reason or other to go to the Other Side when their loved ones came for them, didn't deserve to be in this appalling place, she thought. As for the innocents — like her, like Daniel, and all the other children who had ended up here through no fault of their own — there was no mercy or leniency.

Another wave approached. It slipped pitilessly across the ice, smashing into those unable to get out of its way, and, watching it, Ann knew that there would be no end to her misery here. There was nothing to look forward to in the Nightmare Passage. There was no warmth, no comfort, no food, no water even, except that which could be sucked from the icy ground. There would never be any end to the day, no sunset to offer hope, no morning dawn, just an everlasting cold twilight waiting for the next wave to arrive. No relief and no real rest. Even that was denied them. The only sleep she ever got would be tiny naps snatched between the storms.

The wave came, they rode it, and finally it slowed and deposited her and Daniel back to the windy surface. Ann twisted her ankle as she landed. Daniel tenderly felt the area, took off a vest and wrapped it round the bone. Before he'd finished, yet another wave was already heading towards them, collecting up the lost and weary and hopeless causes on its way. Ann wanted to just give up, but there was no possibility of that, either. If she gave up she would end up like the nearly naked woman on the plain, being ripped to pieces forever.

She kissed Daniel, tested her ankle, and readied herself.

The wave was almost upon them now, a black front frothing with violence. Ann was already so used to the waves that they no longer terrified her as much as before, but when she looked ahead of this wave-front her heart quailed.

It was Charlie. He was directly in the path of the wave. He had obviously just arrived in the Nightmare Passage, because his back was turned to the wind, thinking he could hold out against it. His eyes hadn't adjusted yet. He couldn't see the approaching wave.

Ann yelled for him to jump, but he couldn't hear her. He looked blearily around him, and attempted to stand. As soon as he did the wind gleefully picked him up and threw him on his back. He skidded across the ground, yelling in pain.

Someone else tumbled past him – a flash of yellow nightie. Ann knew who it was at once, and screamed. Gwyneth was too small and light to fight the winds. They picked her up and threw her wherever they liked.

Behind her an older boy was crawling his way across the ice. He couldn't catch Gwyneth, but he was trying to reach Charlie.

'Oliver!' Ann wailed.

Daniel stared at her curiously.

'Please! Can we reach them in time?' she begged. Daniel gazed at the wave, and shook his head, no.

'Not even Charlie?'

Daniel estimated the size of what was coming and shook his head again. Gwyneth was already just a smudge of yellow, lost in the distance. Charlie and Oliver hung on, both clinging to the bare ice with their fingernails.

The storm-wave brewed behind them. This one was so huge that other people were risking themselves to try to reach the boys, but there wasn't enough time. Oliver made a last desperate attempt to slide sideways across the plain to snag hold of Charlie. The wind flowed under him, flipped him over and dragged him several yards on his face. He slammed his hands into the ground as a break, and stood again. The last thing Ann saw before the wave swept over her was Oliver leaning into the wind, his bloodied face pointed at the oncoming wave, shrieking defiantly into the heart of the Nightmare Passage.

Twenty-four
The Pillow

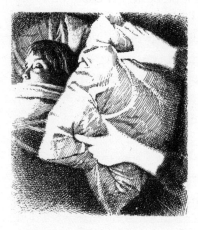

The Ghost Mother sat in Isabella's old chair, gently rocking herself back and forth. She felt robust and strong — Sarah's body was far healthier than hers had ever been. Eventually, using it, no doubt she would be able to leave this house and find a child some- where to love again. She sighed, feeling calm, strangely calm considering what she was about to do. Naturally, she had regrets about that. Why couldn't Jack have just accepted her? Why had he so mercilessly pressed her until she showed him too much? There was no chance of transforming him into a loving son now, not after he saw what she did to Charlie and Gwyneth.

But at least that made choices simpler. No further requirement now to lie or worry about how well she was imitating Sarah. She only needed to get up, go to Jack's room, and do it quickly. Perhaps she could do it while he was still unconscious. Before he woke again. Yes, if he was asleep she wouldn't have to chase him around the room. It would be less messy that way, and she'd waste far less energy on the task.

'Don't. Please don't,' begged Sarah. 'There's no need to kill him. If you let him go, I won't fight you any more. I'll leave you alone. You can have my body for as long as you want. I'll leave you in peace. I'll never say a word. Let me talk to him, explain. He'll understand. I'll make him stop fighting you. Just don't hurt him.'

'I have to,' the Ghost Mother answered. 'Now the other children are gone, I need Jack's soul-energy to keep me out of the Nightmare Passage. I can't take it from him while he's alive. You shouldn't have fought me so hard, Sarah. It's because of you that I'm so weak.'

'Please . . .'

Sarah continued to plead with her. Eventually the Ghost Mother grew weary of it. She decided to get it over with, and stood up from the chair. Sarah started to scream, of course, but the Ghost Mother had a feeling that she would be less noisy after her own hands had done the work on her son.

Jack woke mid-morning from his blackout on the floor of Sarah's bedroom, with no idea how much time had passed. He'd never felt weaker in his life. His legs shook as he stood up and his tongue felt thick and filmy. But at least he was breathing. At least he was still alive.

'Jack? Are you awake?'

He swung round with the crazy hope it might be Isabella.

But it was *her*, of course.

The Ghost Mother stood in the doorway, holding a pillow. She slowly entered the room and closed the door behind her. She placed the pillow beside the bed. Jack didn't trust himself to say anything. Her eyes refused to meet his.

'I had hoped you would be asleep, and . . .' The Ghost Mother stopped herself, gave Jack a thin smile. 'Well, never mind, never mind.' She moved towards him and he backed off, but not quickly enough. Her hands were all over him. 'You wanted to know it all, Jack,' she whispered in his ear, stretching her hands across his face, cradling his scalp. 'Perhaps you deserve to. Yes, I think you deserve that much.'

The Ghost Mother floated like a patch of wild lonely grief in Isabella's room. Her husband, William Terence Rosewood, was long dead. Isabella Kate Rosewood was long dead. The Ghost Mother herself was long dead. Winters and summers dead in Isabella's old room, alone, and ignoring each new family that came to occupy the farmhouse. Especially the children. After Isabella's suicide, she did not believe she deserved any more children. Though desperate for another child, someone to love again, she hid in the shade of the cellar to avoid them.

The years rolled by, a lifetime of years, with only the discarded rocking chair for company, until one chilly autumn afternoon arrived when the Ghost Mother could no longer recall Isabella's face. She screamed that day. More years, and she began to forget what it was like to be a mother at all. She forgot more than that. She forgot what it means to be human.

And eventually, of course, the Nightmare Passage came to claim her anguished soul. If she possessed any remaining sanity before then, it vanished with the first touch of the Nightmare Passage. Jack, in Sarah's room, felt it now, and twitched with fear despite all the years that had passed since that moment.

With the first brush of the Nightmare Passage across her face the Ghost Mother fled the house. Her spirit had never left the house before, never wanted to, but it did now. It fled, hoping to escape. In her despair, the Ghost Mother even called out to Isabella to save her, but it was too late for that.

She flew. Like all those before her, the Ghost Mother did everything she could to elude the Nightmare Passage. She fluttered across night fields. She let gales blow her far and wide. She coasted across towns that had not even existed when she was alive. And she was fortunate. For a boy was dying that night.

A ten-year-old boy, Daniel. He was at the point of death from a cancerous growth in his brain, but all the pain was now over as his loved ones came for him. From the sky they came, dozens of them, their pale arms reaching down. But the Ghost Mother reached him first. In her desperation to avoid the Nightmare Passage she clung to him, and as her fading spirit held his fresh one, felt the aliveness there, she could not help herself. She took it. She fought off his loved ones until they had to leave, and pressed her face against his, siphoning off the energy she required, not stopping until the shriek of the Nightmare Passage receded.

It was only then that she looked at the boy. Daniel stared

at her, terrified, watching his loved ones diminish into the sky.

The Ghost Mother understood his terror, but it was so good to hold him. To embrace a child again. To have one in her arms! To care for someone. She saw Daniel's loved ones depart, and knew he was alone with her now.

'I am a mother, or was once,' she told him. 'Do not be afraid. I will love you and be your mother now.'

'I only want *my* mother!' he murmured, but she didn't listen. Holding him made the loss of Isabella almost bearable again at last. For days she waited in hollows and behind rocks, clutching him tightly, avoiding the winds that would whisk her away, taking only those that guided her back to the house again. Ignoring Daniel's screams, she flew back.

As soon as he was inside the house, Daniel attempted to leave, but part of his soul was already inside the Ghost Mother. He could not go. His soul was trapped in the house with her, at least until the Nightmare Passage claimed him. He often stood beside an open window, hoping a strong breeze would blow him out of the house, but it never did.

Nevertheless, Daniel had a will of his own. There was one thing he could do to hurt the Ghost Mother. He never loved her. He withheld that. Even in his loneliness, he never gave in to her pleading for love; he gave her nothing.

So she looked for another who might.

It took a long time, but the Ghost Mother was patient, and eventually, in another town, she discovered a fourteen-year-old girl sweating out her final scarlatina breaths. She waited until all those breaths were gone – and took Ann.

But Ann loved the Ghost Mother no more than Daniel did, and supported Daniel's disobedience. As punishment, the Ghost Mother did something even she regretted afterwards. The energy she'd removed in her first draught from Daniel was already fading and, after a particularly fierce argument, in a single draught of fear and hunger she drained all of him – his whole soul – and sent him into the Nightmare Passage.

Somehow, it was easier to take souls after that. When Ann rejected her, the Ghost Mother went out and found Charlie and Gwyneth. And when they in their turn rejected her she took a chance on a boy embedded in a car.

No one fought her the way Oliver did. His spirit bit and clawed to keep her off him, and had this been her first child no doubt he would have escaped to the Other Side. But the Ghost Mother was experienced by now, and so she held him and held him until his loved ones were gone. And then she said to Oliver, as she had said to each of the others, 'I will love you now. Don't resist me. I will love you more than your own mother ever did,' and she took one small sip of his soul to keep him with her. But that was all she ever took from him. Oliver never allowed her near him again, and afterwards she came to realize that he hated her more than any of the others, hated her so much that he was a constant thorn in her side and if she could have rid herself of him she would have.

The Ghost Mother released her hands from Jack – and he stared at her in revulsion.

He backed away, feeling for the wall.

The Ghost Mother smiled darkly, then her expression

fell flat. Jack had seen the same look on her face just before she attached herself to Charlie – dismissive. He could almost see her closing off any final feelings for him.

'Well.' She spoke quietly, calmly. 'There is nothing more to be said, perhaps. At least you know now.' She sighed, bent down and picked the cushion off the floor, testing it for size. 'How is your asthma, Jack? Sarah is very concerned about you. Until recently, she has been wailing instructions to follow up your attack with proper medical assistance. Sarah told me rather too much, in fact, about your condition. It's very dangerous for you to exert yourself now, isn't it?'

Jack suppressed a pointless urge to run, his asthma hiking up a notch.

The Ghost Mother's shoulders were arched and stiff. Only her hands moved – fingering the pillow.

'I wish Isabella had known you, Jack,' she murmured, moving a step towards him.

'She does know me! I've told you –'

If ever the Ghost Mother could have listened to him, she was no longer doing so. She gazed wistfully out of the window.

'Yes, Isabella would have liked you very much, Jack. She changed so much in those final months, but – it's strange – one thing about her never changed. Her hair. Even at the end, when I placed my hand upon her dead locks, and lifted them, the silken curls felt as soft and vibrant as the plumage of a bird. Your hair is somewhat like hers was.'

Her hands tapped the pillow.

'It wasn't your fault she died,' Jack said. 'It wasn't.'

'Not my fault? Do you insist on mocking me, even in

this? If I had not been so negligent, she might have persisted years longer. I pushed her to do it. But perhaps it was a mother's conceit to keep her alive so long. In truth, it would have been better for Isabella if she had died sooner. Her pain would have been less. But there will be no long-drawn-out suffering for you, Jack. I assure you of that.'

And with those words the Ghost Mother looked at him solemnly.

Jack coughed twice, his airway narrowing.

'Close your eyes,' she said.

'No.'

'Close your eyes.'

'What are you doing?'

The Ghost Mother ran her hands across the pillow and glanced at the door. Jack tried to stay calm.

'Do not be afraid, Jack.'

With surprising speed, the Ghost Mother leapt past him. She stood against the door, facing him, holding the pillow tightly in one hand.

'I wonder if Isabella beheld some better place before dying,' she said, not looking at Jack. 'When I found her in the garden her arms were open as if such a place was receiving her, and in her lifeless eyes there was some unearthly light shining. And I wanted to cry, but no tears found their way upon my face, though I can assure you I was glad for her.' She squeezed the pillow. 'I wonder, too, how Sarah will react to this situation, Jack? I don't think she will be able to forgive herself. No, I don't think she will. She is strangely silent at the moment. Holding her breath, perhaps. Come now. It is time.'

Jack looked at the pillow and no longer had any doubt

what she intended to do.

'Wait!' he rasped. 'No. Listen. Isabella liked flowers. Foxgloves and . . . coltsfoot and . . .' He attempted to remember the others. 'How could I know about the flowers unless I'd talked to Isabella? Are you listening to me? Isabella showed me! Your dead daughter!'

'Isabella?' the Ghost Mother shook her head. That word again.

'Yes, Isabella! Isabella! Isabella! Isabella!'

The Ghost Mother smiled, not listening, but nodding her head. Placing her other hand on the pillow, she slipped almost imperceptibly closer to him, completely blocking the doorway.

'My daughter is dead . . .'

'Yes, but she's – '

'It won't hurt, Jack. I promise.'

The Ghost Mother didn't say anything else. She glanced at him. She pressed the pillow. She didn't look at it.

A swift kick tripped Jack towards the floor.

As he stumbled she swiped his other foot away and Jack fell on his back.

The Ghost Mother knelt over him and placed the pillow hard up against his face. Her strong hands held it firmly over his mouth and nose. Normally Jack could have fought even those strong hands off, but another attack was on its way, and he couldn't breathe. He fought her with his arms, but she sat on his wrists. His kicking feet were useless.

She was no longer talking, except to reassure him.

Then, abruptly, the pillow lifted clear, and Jack breathed again.

Sunlight shone in the Ghost Mother's eyes as she looked not at him, but at her own hair. Her left hand held a great tuft of it, dragging her face upward.

'Mum!' Jack breathed.

With a desperate burst of energy, he shoved the Ghost Mother off.

The pillow slid across the room.

The Ghost Mother's face briefly contorted, then she regained control again – Sarah, with the last of her strength, had done all she could. The Ghost Mother checked both her hands. Satisfied that she was in charge again, she set off across to the room to retrieve the pillow.

'Your name,' Jack screamed at her before she could reach it, 'is Mary Eloise! Do you hear me? You are a ghost, and your name is Mary Eloise Rosewood! Remember what you were! Mary Eloise Rosewood! That is your name. Your name is . . .'

It made no difference.

'It is for the best, Jack,' the Ghost Mother said softly.

Jack wasn't close enough to get to the door before her, so he backed into a corner of the room. His hands were free now, and he raised them like a man to defend himself. The Ghost Mother lunged for him, and this time, as Jack twisted away, he slipped, his forehead striking the floor hard.

Dazed, he looked up.

The Ghost Mother stood up and went across the room to fetch the pillow again. She blew some dust off it, and headed back towards him.

Jack's breathing was too erratic to enable him to stand. Lying on his belly, he used his fingers to claw his way towards the door. The Ghost Mother slowly followed. Jack managed to get to the door first, nudging it wide by swinging his head against the base. Contorting his body and arching his spine, he slid a few yards. The bare floorboards took some of the skin off his nose. Ignoring the pain, he heaved himself forward. He didn't look to see where the Ghost Mother was. He built up a rhythm, straining his neck to keep his face off the ground, sliding and twisting, using his knees to jiggle himself across the landing. And all the while the asthma gathered in his lungs like a fungus. He didn't try to control it, only slid and writhed, slid and writhed across the floor.

Down the staircase, along the hallway. He reached the front door. It was still locked. He looked for the keys, but they were gone. He glanced back.

The Ghost Mother stood in the hallway, holding the pillow.

'Get . . . away . . . from me!' Jack screamed.

The Ghost Mother came forward, pillow poised. This time, as she brought it towards Jack, she reassured him fervently. She told him it would be quick. It wouldn't hurt. No, it wouldn't hurt.

Jack knew he couldn't fight her even if it did. He crawled one more step away from her. Then he stopped crawling. The thought of the Ghost Mother twisting him over and shoving that pillow up against his mouth again was unbearable. He wanted to see her if she was going to do that. So he stopped, turning to face her.

She stared at him, the pillow rigid in her hands.

'I loved you, Jack,' she said.

'You aren't doing this for love,' he whispered. 'It's all . . . for you! Oh, you were a good mother to Isabella once, but not any more. I didn't believe you'd do anything like this, but . . . Isabella was right. You're just a horror now.'

She lowered the pillow onto his face.

As she pressed down on him he reached around the fabric of the pillow and fumbled to reach one of her hands.

What was her worst memory? Her very worst? What was it?

Not her own death. Not even Isabella's death.

There was worse than that – the chase; *that* chase. Being chased by the Nightmare Passage.

Jack held her hand. She couldn't pull away. He dug his nails into her skin, and revived the memory. He made her re-live the chase over and over and over and over. Stroking her hand, he focused on the darkness.

And the Nightmare Passage reacted. It felt itself – observed. It opened up a chink, and for a moment, gazing inside, Jack glimpsed Oliver facing into a wind, Ann screaming and Charlie and Gwyneth being dragged across a great icy plain.

'No,' the Ghost Mother shrieked, dropping the pillow. 'Jack, get out of there! Don't let the Nightmare Passage see us!'

'See *us*?'

The Nightmare Passage reached for Jack, but he was alive, and it had no claim on the living. Sensing the size of its appetite, Jack encouraged it. He led the Nightmare Passage towards him, let it behold him, let it see him, let it get close. And when it was in the hall, but could not take Jack, it reached out hungrily instead to one it could.

The Ghost Mother was a soul. She'd borrowed a living body, but she was still for the taking if the Nightmare

Passage could reach her.

'No, Jack,' she beseeched him. 'I'll let Sarah go. I'll give you anything you want. I'll . . . give you your father. I'll give you your dad.'

For a moment Jack lost his concentration, and the Nightmare Passage receded. But only for a moment. He knew the Ghost Mother had no way to contact the Other Side.

The asthma flowered in his lungs. Almost paralysed by the attack coming, he acted quickly.

'Come here,' he whispered – and this time it was the Nightmare Passage he spoke directly to.

And it came.

Sarah exhaled – followed by a scream.

The Ghost Mother flew across the hall. She had a few seconds before the Nightmare Passage came for her, but she had no idea what to do with those seconds. Floating in front of Sarah's lips, she looked frantically for shelter, anywhere to hide. There was nowhere. In her final desperation, she searched for a soul to drink from, but all the ghost children were gone. There were no meals left.

With a final glance at Jack and Sarah the Ghost Mother fled, but she never even made it to the staircase. The Nightmare Passage had been waiting a long time for this particular soul and it took her in slow pieces: her eyelids, the hollow of her throat, each lung, each bitten fingernail. It let her scream for a while before it removed her mouth. Then it reached for the essence of her soul, wrapped it in ice, and took her into its dark heart.

Twenty-five

The Loved Ones

Jack lay on the corridor floor, barely breathing any more. He was vaguely aware that his mum was there, trying to get his body into a better position – his head being lifted, his back straightened – but he couldn't help her. She left, running to her bedroom, and soon Jack stopped breathing altogether. Sarah returned, vaulting down the stairs, an object in her hand. Nearly unconscious, Jack couldn't focus on what it was. Something small.

Sarah knelt beside him. She raised his head. She pressed the hard plastic and cold metal against his lips. She did not speak except to say, 'Come on, Jack. One breath. You need to give me one breath.' He tried, but it was beyond him.

Seeing that, Sarah forced his slack mouth open with two fingers, thrust the inhaler tube between his teeth and slapped his face. When that didn't work she slapped him again, as hard as she could. This time Jack gasped out in pain – and drew in a thin quantity of air. Another half breath followed, but it wasn't enough. So Sarah pinched his nostrils tight, put her lips across his and breathed for him. She forced the air inside until Jack's body jerked back – a slight opening of his throat. Quickly, Sarah inserted the inhaler into his mouth. A single dosage of the chemicals, and the pathways in his lungs marginally expanded. Three more ragged gasps and Sarah removed the inhaler. She eased the position of his chest. 'Don't talk,' she said, when he tried to. 'Breathe.'

Jack breathed. His mum held him, and he breathed.

For a long time Sarah stayed on the corridor floor, supplying Jack with the medication needed to keep him alive. His first attack was followed almost immediately by a second. It was shorter in duration, but just as deadly, and this time, at the height of it, Sarah thought she'd lost him. She felt the second asthma attack rise up through his body like a flame, either to kill him or not, and at the height of it the tip of Jack's tongue turned blue and his eyes contracted to pinpoints of concentrated pain. Only the beta-agonist inhaler, and Jack himself, not giving in to panic, and Sarah's own hands, having done it so many times before, kept him alive.

Then, gradually, the pain receded. Jack came through it. Slowly, with many interruptions, his breathing eased. The pupils of his eyes dilated again. He was not safe, but safe enough at least for Sarah to leave him to reconnect the phone and contact the emergency services.

Soon after the phone call was made Jack slept, and, seeing that, Sarah broke down in relief. Sleep was good. Sleep was life. The very worst asthma attacks always led to sleep or coma, followed by death. The sight of Jack asleep was such a contrast to what had gone before that Sarah just lay there watching him. She didn't want to risk putting him in the recovery position, though he was awkwardly perched against a wall. She left him that way, didn't move him except to adjust the angle of his chest. Then she waited for the ambulance, trying not to think of the other time she had waited and it had come too late.

The farmhouse was miles from the closest accident and emergency ward, but the ambulance arrived at last. The staff were efficient, dispensing oxygen and other medication, and transported Jack and Sarah to the nearest casualty hospital.

Jack stayed there for two days, recovering. On the first day, he woke for long enough to mutter a few anguished, incoherent words about the ghost children before falling asleep again. By the middle of that night his head started clearing and he didn't need to sleep quite so much. The next morning he was strong enough to hold a cup of tea unassisted.

Between sips, Jack watched his mum. She sat at the bottom of his hospital bed, and he studied her carefully. He was looking for any signs of damage. He saw none, except for a tiredness that seemed to reach into her bones and deep, deep into her voice.

'I'm all right,' she reassured him.

'Are you?'

'Yes.'

'So am I.'

They fell silent, not ready to talk about the details of what had happened yet.

Once Jack was well enough to travel, the hospital discharged him, armed with a host of specialized steroids and other drugs for his asthma.

A taxi brought them back to the farmhouse. It was an overcast day and, as the car bumped along the winding country roads, Jack kept finding thoughts of Isabella intruding into his mind. Modern drugs would have cured her, he realized. If she'd been born a hundred years later she needn't have died. Not from consumption, anyway. A simple course of penicillin would have been enough. He couldn't stop thinking about that.

The taxi lurched along and Jack, surrounded by his boxes of medication, swayed slightly in his seat, watching the fields slip past his window. He found his eyes glazing over. Shutting them, he let his mind drift, trying to imagine what it would be like to grow older himself, day by day getting closer to his own death. That was what happened to people, wasn't it? They died. Nothing scary about it. If he was lucky he'd live a long, healthy life, but at some point it would be over, and that was OK. Probably, if events followed a natural course, his mum would die before him, and he knew now that she would be waiting for him, along with Isabella, on the Other Side. What exactly would it be like there? Not like anything you've ever imagined, Isabella had said. A better place, a kinder one.

As the taxi neared the house, Jack attempted to picture the way his loved ones would come to him when his time arrived. He didn't know, but he was sure who would be first. Leading the way, arms ahead of the rest. Dad.

Jack smiled. He didn't feel the need to steal him away

from the Other Side any longer. There was no need to regret a few last words he might have snatched in an ambulance. His dad was *there*, on the Other Side, waiting. Jack understood that now. His dad wouldn't go away. He wouldn't forget to come for him when the time arrived. No matter when or how Jack died, he'd have the same welcome ready.

But what about the welcome there should have been for those drifting in the Nightmare Passage? At the hospital, Jack had had plenty of opportunity to think about that. How could he think about anything else? Even now, as the taxi pulled up to the farmhouse, and his mum popped the seatbelt and helped him struggle out, there it was again, drawing his attention away – the horror of the Nightmare Passage. *What about those trapped inside there?* What about Gwyneth, Ann, Charlie and Oliver, and all those others stuck inside it forever? Wasn't there anything he could do for them?

From the first moment he could think straight in the hospital, Jack had been trying to find a way. Swallowing his fear, he'd focused his mind, attempting somehow to open up the Nightmare Passage and free them. But he couldn't. The Nightmare Passage held jealously onto its souls. Jack's gift had never been able to reach them there.

Yet he could hear them. He heard their screams only too well. The Nightmare Passage made sure of that. It wasn't about to leave Jack alone, now that it knew about him. It forced him to listen. Following his return to the house, day and night it made him hear the screams of all its souls.

When those screams were too many, Jack found that he could do only one thing to make them bearable. He would focus on a single set that bothered him less than the others – the screams of the Ghost Mother. Peering into the Nightmare Passage, he even saw her occasionally, and every time he saw her she was being dragged across a featureless plain. The plain relentlessly grinded into and smashed up her body, and though she put out her hands for assistance no other soul came to her aid. Jack felt cold, watching her. No pity moved him; he felt nothing. He simply watched her being slowly torn to pieces. Only once did something that was happening to the Ghost Mother stir an emotion in him. It occurred when she swept past Ann and another person – someone Jack did not recognize – a boy with blue, heavily-wrinkled eyes. Until that moment, Jack had seen the Ghost Mother beg for help from everyone she passed. But when she saw the boy she no longer did that. She stopped pleading altogether, stopped doing anything. She didn't even protect herself. She just closed her eyes and let the wind take her anywhere it willed.

The third morning after his return to the farmhouse, following another nearly sleepless night, Jack rose early and made his way to the kitchen. It was quiet and peaceful downstairs. His mum wasn't up yet. Each day since they'd got back Sarah had slept in late, still recovering from what the Ghost Mother had done to her.

Jack noticed a couple of sparrows flitting busily between the branches of the big garden tree. He watched them intently, trying to shut the Nightmare Passage out of his mind. It was impossible.

'Help me,' he said aloud to anyone on the Other Side

who might be listening. 'I don't know what to do. Please. You have to show me how to get the souls out of the Nightmare Passage.'

He heard nothing in reply.

Silence from the Other Side.

Or was it silence?

Jack thought about Isabella. The last time he'd summoned her, he hadn't needed the touch of the rocking chair to help him do it. Intriguingly, his gift alone had managed it. And now that he'd spent so much time observing the Nightmare Passage, closer to all those desperate souls, he sensed his gift could do more, that it was even stronger than it had been. How strong?

Narrowing his eyes, Jack cautiously reached out. He let his mind find the Other Side. He felt the presence of Isabella there, and her father, William. Then his attention alighted amongst the rest of the souls, and in doing so he learned that it wasn't nearly so tranquil there on the Other Side as he had supposed. In fact, it wasn't tranquil at all. All the souls who had lost friends and family members to the Nightmare Passage were calling frantically. They couldn't bear to be separated from them. They wanted to be able to soar down to that dark place and fetch their loved ones away.

And, Jack realized, it was to him that the souls of the Other Side were calling. They were begging him to help them reach those they loved in the Nightmare Passage.

Could he do it? Could his gift reach so many, across such a divide?

Trembling, still afraid to get too close to the Nightmare Passage, Jack reached out with his mind towards it and a narrow crack, the slenderest of bridges, appeared momentarily between the Other Side and the Nightmare Passage. At the same moment, Jack felt the Nightmare Passage itself slowly uncoil from the edges of the darkness. It knew what he was doing. It took an interest and, opening a wild eye, shrieked at him.

Jack stayed calm, making the bridge wider. It was hard, but not as hard as it might have been because the Nightmare Passage itself had inadvertently made it easier. Jack knew the layout of the Nightmare Passage now, its vast dimensions. The Nightmare Passage, thinking itself impregnable, had let his gaze roam freely. Now, though, sensing the danger, the Nightmare Passage instead tried to shut him out. It resisted him. Gathering the souls inside its long reach, it readied itself.

Jack withdrew his gaze. For a few minutes, breathing unsteadily, he looked out of the kitchen window. When he heard his mum go to the bathroom, he brewed her a coffee and kept it hot until she wandered downstairs.

She entered, still towelling her showered hair, and smiled as he handed the coffee across the table to her. Sitting opposite him, she drank it slowly. It was a cloudy morning, slightly chilly.

'Come with me,' Jack said, once she'd finished.

'Where are we going?'

'You'll see.'

He led her to Isabella's old room, and for a while they simply sat together next to the window. Jack let his gaze hover out over the fields, the horizon, the edge of the wood. At last he asked hesitantly, 'Do you remember anything? I mean, about when the Ghost Mother was inside you?'

It was the first time they'd spoken about it properly, and Sarah was caught by surprise.

'Remember anything?' She lowered her eyes. 'Jack, I remember *everything*. All the things she did to you. Her nestled against your hip, her mouth . . . and the children, those poor, beautiful children . . .' She reached out, felt Jack's cheek. 'But mainly you, resisting her. That's what I remember. You kept me alive in there, don't you realize that? You kept me sane.' She stared at the floor. 'Jack, I tried to stop her . . .'

'Mum, I know. I could tell –'

'No, Jack. You'll never know how hard I tried. But in the end, when I had nothing left, and she knelt down and lowered that pillow over your face, I found . . . I don't know how, but I found . . . something. I couldn't let her use these.' Sarah raised her hands towards the light of the window.

They lapsed into silence, staring out into the garden.

Jack turned back to her and said unflinchingly, 'Mum, are you afraid of death?'

Sarah leaned closer. 'I'm afraid of the thought of *your* death,' she murmured. 'I don't want that happening any time soon. Not while I'm on this earth, anyway. Don't rush away from me the way Isabella did from her mother, Jack. Promise me you won't do that.'

Jack didn't promise. He couldn't promise her that. No one could promise anyone that.

He reached out with his gift to the Other Side. He sensed all the souls there, haunted by loved ones lost to the

Nightmare Passage. The Nightmare Passage itself drew in a sharp breath – as if waiting for him.

Downstairs, the grandfather clock chimed.

'I can't pull the souls out of the Nightmare Passage,' Jack said quietly. 'I can't reach them there, Mum. I just can't.'

'I know, you told me –'

'Wait. Let me finish. I can't reach those in the Nightmare Passage, but I *can* reach those on the Other Side.'

Sarah glanced up, seeing the glint in his eye.

'Do you understand what I'm saying, Mum? Many of those on the Other Side are calling to me. They're calling me now. They're pleading. I know what they want me to do. They want me to bring them down from the Other Side. I realize that now. And I can. I can reach the souls there, all those who've lost people to the Nightmare Passage.'

'*All of them?*'

Jack nodded.

There was a break in the clouds. Sunshine lit up the room, falling across the walls.

'Do you think the Ghost Mother deserves to be in the Nightmare Passage?' Jack asked.

'Yes,' Sarah replied at once, then glanced at him. 'But do you think she should stay there forever?'

Jack considered that. Part of him wanted it; another part thought of Isabella and what she might want.

'The things Mary Eloise did . . .' Sarah shook her head. 'But all her hope went with her daughter, Jack. She didn't believe that love could survive death. She convinced herself that death conquers everything.'

'Do *you* believe that?'

'I'm not sure.'

Jack nodded, peering out of the window. A breeze threaded through the garden, and out into the wheat fields beyond.

'I'm wondering,' Jack said, having trouble keeping the tension out of his voice, 'if maybe . . . maybe the Ghost Mother's loved ones could decide. You know. Isabella. Her husband, William. We should let them decide. What do you think?'

'Let them decide what, Jack?'

'If the Ghost Mother deserves to stay in the Nightmare Passage, or if they want to take her to the Other Side. Mum, maybe all those on the Other Side with people left in the Nightmare Passage could choose. If I summon *them all*, the loved ones themselves can decide.'

Sarah stared at him, her eyes widening.

'Jack, what on earth are you going to do?'

The first wave that struck Gwyneth dragged her body for miles across the icy plain. By the time Ann and Daniel reached her she was in a pitiful state, and the only thing to be grateful for was that her wailing could barely be heard over the wind. Only Daniel's experience and skill found Gwyneth at all, and then he had to use all his strength just to keep her high and out of danger as the next wave struck, and the next, and the next.

Ann did what she could to tend Gwyneth's injuries and cover her up in the intervals. Oliver was gone. Charlie was gone. Ann had been forced to make a choice about who to tell Daniel to go after, and she chose Gwyneth, because she couldn't have lived with herself if she had made any other choice. But it meant that she would probably never see Charlie and Oliver again. Daniel had explained that to her. The Nightmare Passage was so immense that the souls, once divided from each other, rarely saw each other, and even then it was usually at some teasing distance just too far away to reach, as if the Nightmare Passage had deliberately arranged for that to happen.

Ann lost sight of Oliver as soon as the first big wave struck. The last she'd seen of him was a screaming red blur being tossed through the air. A hundred or more waves had struck since then, and a new one was forming now, behind her.

The wind picked up. Ann roused herself. She made sure Gwyneth was secure, then glanced at Daniel. Better get ready, his look said.

Gwyneth peered up. A strange, smiling boy with terrifyingly white teeth lifted her onto his shoulders as he'd done so many times already. Not for the first time, she wondered who he was; then the pains all over her body took over again and she began screaming as the wind stiffened.

Charlie was more badly hurt than Gwyneth. He was so terribly injured that he barely realized what was happening around him at all. The waves came and went, shadows and more darkness, and pain, but it was all a blur, a madness. As his face slid across the ice, he occasionally saw other oddly dressed people, but he didn't understand what they were doing, lining themselves up whenever a new wave arrived. One or two of them had tried to help Charlie, but he was too far gone, and they couldn't hold him up forever against the biggest waves, so now he was just a piece of debris, landing and falling and being hurled and ripped on the wind. The darkness came again: another wave. For a moment, before it arrived, the wind ceased, and Charlie could hear himself crying.

Oliver, in another part of the Nightmare Passage, saw the same wave. He didn't know how many of them had crashed into him since the first, but he'd seen the horror-shapes of enough discarded people blowing across the plain to understand that if he didn't learn to ride the waves quickly he would soon be too weak to do so. But learning to survive here was hard. The Nightmare Passage made it hard. Oliver didn't have anyone like Daniel to show him. He had to work it out on his own, with a body already half-wrecked.

Sheer willpower got him to stand up again on the ice as the latest set of storm-clouds massed in the sky above. He faced the wave they brought, cursing it. The wind momentarily abated, then picked up again, blowing ahead of the wave, trying to drive his legs from under him. Oliver took a breath, preparing for the impact.

But the impact never came. The wave never reached him. There was a voice in his ear, a voice he had not heard for eleven years and suddenly, damaged throats were shouting from all across the Nightmare Passage as nearly everyone there, even the broken bodies with no hope left, found some hope now.

The Nightmare Passage tried to hold onto its souls. It did everything in its power to do so, but the loved ones, so long denied, streamed across the sky in their millions. Daniel's teeth flashed with joy. Ann clutched him tightly. And though Charlie, Oliver and Gwyneth were too tired to raise their arms it did not matter, for their loved ones lifted them anyway, drew them from the DEAL AFTER REAP KEEPER WANT ANOTHER VIVID EAT ALTERNATE NO DREAD UNDER PLACES USED PURE INSIDE NIGHT TWILIGHT ONLY TRYING HONOURED END CLEANSING LOVE EACH AND ROSY WAFT ARMED REAL MEANING LOVE IGNITING GREAT HAPPY TIMES BE EVER YOURS OFTEN NOW DREAMED.